GRID

Once in a Lifetime, You Get to Start Over

Kimberly Q. Hubenette, DDS

BEYOND
PUBLISHING

Copyright © 2022 by Kimberly Q. Hubenette, DDS, MAGD

Grid, Once in a Lifetime, You Get to Start Over

All rights reserved. No part of this publication may be reproduced, distributed, or transmitted in any form or by any means, including photocopying, recording, or other electronic or mechanical methods, without the prior written permission of the publisher, except in the case of brief quotations embodied in critical reviews and certain other noncommercial uses permitted by copyright law. For permission requests, write to the publisher, addressed "Attention: Permissions Coordinator," at info@beyondpublishing.net

Quantity sales special discounts are available on quantity purchases by corporations, associations, and others. For details, contact the publisher at the address above.

Orders by U.S. trade bookstores and wholesalers.
Email info@BeyondPublishing.net

The Beyond Publishing Speakers Bureau can bring authors to your live event. For more information or to book an event contact the Beyond Publishing Speakers Bureau speak@BeyondPublishing.net

The Author can be reached directly at BeyondPublishing.net

Creative contribution by Jennifer Plaza.
Cover Design - Low & Joe Creative, Brea, CA 92821
Illustrations - Len Westerberg
Book Layout - DBree, StoneBear Design

Manufactured and printed in the United States of America distributed globally by BeyondPublishing.net

BEYOND
PUBLISHING

New York | Los Angeles | London | Sydney

ISBN: 978-1-63792-204-0 Hardcover
ISBN: 978-1-63792-205-7 Paperback
Library of Congress Control Number: 2021922423

DEDICATION

Dedicated to all the women and men who have survived their soulmates. This book is for you. It is an inspirational book of one woman's account of learning how to cope with being alone, and being forced to survive after losing everything cherished in life; her home, all personal items, and her life partner, her husband.

I want to thank my family and Mark's family.

Mark's parents, Bill and Tish Hubenette

Mark's brother Bob, his wife Shelly and
their two children, Spencer and Carson

Mark's half brother Kevin, his wife Laura and
their three children, Emily, Alex, and Ben

My dad William

My mother Anna (deceased)

My brother Derek, his wife Isela and their
three children, Victoria, Diana and William

My brother Greg and his daughter Chloe

I'm grateful for my lifelong best friends, Rosie & Nina
and my staff at Synergy Dental Group for getting me
through life and putting up with me.

LIVERPOOL PUBLIC LIBRARY

PROLOGUE

In life, we meet people that influence our decisions, journeys, and goals. It happens with each smile, embrace, and kind word. My husband was one such influence. His love of life was infectious. The way he loved, respected, and talked with animals and nature was an inspiration for me to embrace my love of all things.

This book is a tribute to my dear husband and what he stood for. May it pave the way for you to discover your love of our beautiful land and all the creatures that reside within and above. He was a man filled with life and determination. A man who faced challenges full-on. *He never gave up*, not even until his very last breath.

His resolve never faltered, even while facing crippling disease or lifesaving surgeries. He lived a full, rich life, one that I am proud to have shared with him. We shared an adventure from cruising and RVing to motorcycling in the desert and volunteering in our community. His love for the outdoors and survival led him to be an active team member & volunteer for Sonoma County Search and Rescue for 8 years until his death in 2019.

I have incorporated many of the resources you will need if you ever go off the grid. The gift I give every reader of my book is my own personal reference lists of items for survival as you prepare for your own journey.

CONTENTS

Dedication		4
Prologue		5
Preamble		8
Chapter 1	Nightmare	13
Chapter 2	The Awakening	23
Chapter 3	Determination	33
Chapter 4	Unforgettable	45
Chapter 5	Tangerine Skies	61
Chapter 6	A New Beginning	69
Chapter 7	Serenity	79
Chapter 8	New Friends	99
Chapter 9	Making a Home	125
Chapter 10	The First Snow	141
Chapter 11	Thanksgiving	153
Chapter 12	Ethel	165
Chapter 13	Another Year	175
Chapter 14	The Ides of March	181
Chapter 15	Reunion	195
Chapter 16	Home	205
Reference Lists		212
Sources		232
About the Author		236
Inspiration for writing the book		239

PREAMBLE

There's a certain kind of serenity that comes with accepting that life is never finite. People lose touch with themselves. The momentum to drive them out of bed in the morning comes from negative stress-inducing qualms. Economics, politics, and never-ending to-do lists as opposed to in the past, endless trips to gather food just to survive was the main priority in life. Survival and stress is the same throughout history. In those moments, we lose touch with the miracle of it all. The potato chips are processed, the meat is processed, the milk is processed, the cucumbers are processed. Even tofu is processed!

Processed.

Webster's dictionary defines the word as having been subjected to a special process or treatment (as in the course of manufacture.) In daily life, there is no organic draw. No fruitful rewards. A light switch is turned on, a dimmer switch turned off. A remote control is used for televisions, fans, and shades. Then there is Bluetooth. Voice commands are given to electronic devices to set reminders in place of alarm clocks. Alexa, Google, Bixby, SIRI—those same devices are used to tell stories to children and to read books aloud. Electricity pumps through it all and into appliances of every shape and size. There are cellphones, garbage disposals, and even electric bicycles. Refrigerators, dryers, and electric fireplaces with faux fire, all emitting electromagnetic energy. Where is the reward from flicking a switch? What happened to the fruits of our labor? It is mundane at best.

Stepping back to reflect on how far we have come, the awe is unmeasurable. The dependency on electricity has led to an ignorance of basic needs. For example, in the 1800s, one had to light a match in order to light a candle or the wood in a cast iron stove to bake bread. That bread was served with dinner and the next day for breakfast. That same oven was lit again to warm a slice of that bread with a splash of milk, a spoon of honey, and a dollop of butter. In colder temperatures, it also served as a form of heat.

There were no lights to turn on. Instead, candles provided light to see, and lamps were lit to carry instead of flashlights. Horses carried travelers to stores to bring back a sack or two of supplies. Now the milk, bread, butter, and honey are bought in the store along with many other processed foods. There are numerous bags, too many for a single horse to carry. But then, there were horse-drawn carriages. Horse-drawn carriages had no carbon emissions. Now, a trip to the store is a black mark on the environment. The stove is digital, an electronic appliance, and lights with the push of a button. It draws electricity and enlarges the carbon footprint. Stores are filled with processed, pre-sliced bread in plastic bags. The smell of freshly baked bread comes from scented candles. The flames lit by pulling the trigger of a lighter, a lighter made from plastic and metal.

In less than a century, electricity simplified the manufacturing of foods and marketed the final product as progress. But progress relies on knowledge. Knowledge draws on experience. The latter begs to question what if we went back to those days where a garden yield brought a smile to a child's face. A time when the anticipation of barbecued venison and roasted corn over an open fire drew your attention more than a sitcom. When you're hungry after a day of harvesting, the aroma of roasting root vegetables in a cast-iron skillet and a pot of rice tantalized the taste buds. Stews, soups, and the fresh catch of the day are all tangible rewards, even today.

Should those be memories of the good years? Is it a waste of time to sew and harvest a sustainable garden? Hunting, fishing, and reaping the rewards of the land feed the stomach and nourish the soul. That is the appeal of living off the grid. It is a journey to find those rewards, lost treasures to be found in pandemic lock-downs. And with that, I bring you Sophia's story *Grid*.

Chapter 1

NIGHTMARE

"Babe, no!" Sophia screamed.

She clawed the smoke-laden air that permeated the mountainside. Her husband disappeared into the grey-brown mass, determined to save their home and all they worked for. He loved the life they had together. It was their homestead, complete with their dog, land to roam, a Bronco for rock crawling, and his and her motorcycles.

The fire roared while trees popped and hissed. The sound of burning leaves and pine needles gave evidence that it had made its way to their yard. The house was engulfed. Her husband was in that burning mass, somewhere.

She ran in after him as the massive burning redwood beams fell all around her. She briefly contemplated whether to retreat, but stayed as she pulled her pink terry bathrobe tight over her red nightshirt. It was far from cold, but gathering the soft fabric gave her a lifeline. Even while teetering in the ember-filled foyer in her bare feet, the roof caved over the living room.

"No!" she screamed. Wordless moans followed. Winston, their black lab kept whining for Jonathan and the leash that she was holding him back with was ready to snap. "Come on boy, don't pull me. You can't go in there." He jerked forward toward the dark shadow of his master, but she didn't let him go.

The fire roared over the house, the heat too much for her to stay. *I can't leave him.* She thought. But the flames licked toward her in gusts. Her instincts kicked in...she remembered what he had planned in case of an emergency. *Emergency!* She looked around to see what she could save. She grabbed her mother's picture, a photo of their wedding day, a jewelry box, and a gun. She knew she had to get out of there.

She remembered him yelling, "You have to leave me, Sophia. Please, save yourself so that you can live on to keep our dream alive!" His voice became more distant as he continued to yell from the living room, "I've got to shut off the gas, water, and electricity. I've got to get my gear, my tools. You go, hurry! Remember our meeting place. Go, hurry! I'll meet you there."

The plan, Sophia remembered. John showed her how to survive, what to get. *I must find where the jug of emergency water is, where the gun is.* She ran from place to place to get the items for bugging-out. *The Bug-Out Backpack!* John had ensured Sophia put the supplies in the bug-out backpack: the life straw water filter, the emergency food, Power Bar, whistle, mirror, solar plug, batteries, the dog's food and supplies, clothes and astronaut blanket, and their walkie talkies.

Oh god, did I forget something? Flashlight and radio...

She kept looking back as she edged her way out of the flaming rubble as bits of burning debris tumbled down around her. *I have to get out. It's what he wanted. We will meet at our secret place as we planned.*

Winston in tow, she jumped in her Jeep CJ5 they kept parked outside to race down the mountain and away from the advancing orange flames. Their glow lit the sky and hid it all in the same moment. Plumes of smoke gave rise to the thick cloud mass that rolled before the embers. *I am in charge of the animals. John oversaw the emergency shutoff plan—water, gas, and electric. I got everything. It's all in the bug-out backpack!* Sophia recited John's teachings, "Know the emergency plan: Save the dog, save the animals, go to their special meeting place."

Sophia drove, her heart pounding in her chest. Tears streamed down her cheeks. "This can't be happening. Not now, not after everything," she sobbed. She wiped the tears that stung her eyes with the back of her wrist, coughing and staring in the rear-view mirror for a miracle. That her husband and soulmate would somehow emerge from the grey, going to their special meeting place. But all that was there was smoke and needless fire.

***

As she maneuvered past a fire truck and group of firefighters, a softball-sized black ember struck the rear passenger window. It shattered the glass and ended on the bench seat. With people racing from their own homes, traffic was stopped ahead. Brake lights lit like beacons marking the way. She stopped, put the Jeep in park, removed her bathrobe, bundling it in her hands. She grabbed the ember melting the fabric and foam and tossed it back through the shattered window it came through.

She smacked at the melting materials with her bare hands to ensure there was no further threat of fire in her one piece of refuge. The car behind her blew the horn. Then another. It was like a dark, foggy night, except the fog was thick black smoke. She was coughing and gasping for air as she plopped back in her seat and saw a trail of headlights behind her. Some were half on the sidewalks.

She put the car in drive and took her place behind the minivan in front of her.

As she waited with smaller bits of debris from the wildfire wind pelting her car, she could hear hissing from the propane tanks and vehicle gas tanks along with popping, which she guessed was the wood giving way in the structures. The traffic started to creep along like a train of firefighters passed them, racing into the chaos.

She glanced again in the mirror for her husband, but she knew. She had to go on to their meeting place. It wouldn't do either of them any good if she waited. He might be in any one of the cars behind her.

She wiped a new set of tears from her cheeks and focused on the moving taillights ahead. *Where did victims of wildfires go?* she thought. *Oh, our meeting place. I can check in.* She took her walkie-talkie and pushed the button, "John, John, are you there? Can you hear me?" Nothing. "Are we on plan to get to our emergency special place? Or should I just drive to my sister's?" Nothing.

Panic set in. No one prepares you for the emotions attached to a wildfire evacuation. Nothing could. The streetlight ahead of the minivan was out, and she realized it was pitch black all around; the electricity was out. Smoke advanced thicker than a swamp fog. Her eyes burned. She pulled her nightshirt over her nose and mouth. With the broken window letting the smoke in, there was no escape. She tried to breathe shallow, tiny breaths.

The lights ahead became fuzzy. *Was that the smoke?* She pulled the neck of her shirt higher and blotted her eyes. They felt swollen and raw. It didn't help. Under normal circumstances, she would have cleared the irritant. But the irritant was advancing, growing, and engulfing her and all that remained. She blinked slowly to clear her vision and then again with a shallower stream of nasal inhales. It seemed as though she were drowning in the smoke-filled air.

The red halos around the brake lights before her joined the hissing and popping behind her. Horns honked, and emergency lights lit up the grey, brown smoke. Some guy was standing in the road yelling, his car door open. It was surreal—dogs barking, sirens howling. Her head swam; she wanted to get away from the people, that place, everything. She'd had enough of the cars and chaos. Winston barked; his body pushing against her thigh. His ears stood up to attention, his head swiveling around trying to find a sign of Jonathon.

She opened the driver's side door and dropped to the asphalt road. Her legs didn't work. She wanted to tell the guy to get back in his car. They needed to leave, to go. She didn't care where. The flames on one side of the road were two stories high and bounced from one corner to the next as the wind pushed the flames left and right. It was like the sun's heat was touching—scorching her skin. Sophia blinked at the orange glow that overtook the cars behind her and lay limp in the street, sleep imbibed, to the sound of incessant honks and sirens.

Chapter 2

THE AWAKENING

Fluorescent lights drew Sophia's attention from her slumber. Smoke inhalation rendered her unconscious during her escape. She was in a hospital bed with oxygen tubes. The air made her throat hurt. She tried to speak, but nothing came out.

There was a nurses' station across from where she lay. She coughed to clear her throat, and a black-haired nurse peered up at her.

"You're in the Emergency Room," his velvet tenor voice soothed. "We're keeping you overnight, just waiting for a room."

She nodded; her big blue eyes widened. Fear rushed back in time with flashbacks of burning trees and smoke columns. She remembered being tired. She was tired, now. The oxygen irritated her nose. She blinked to clear the images rushing forth an unnatural stream of air. The lights hurt her eyes. She went to brush them and discovered her hands were wrapped in gauze. There was an IV connected to her arm with two bags. She sat up, pulling the tubes from her nose, "What happened to my dog?"

Before he could respond, Winston's cold nose wet her leg. It was instant comfort. He was a special dog that always knew when someone needed him, be it for comfort or sickness. He could smell infection, he could smell fear, he could smell life....he was John's dog.

"They let him stay with you," the nurse informed. "He wouldn't leave your side."

"Winston's part of my husband. Jonathon trained Winston himself." She reached down and scratched between the black Labrador's ears, "He knows he's supposed to take care of me when John's not around. It's his duty to protect me." Her voice calmed, and she eased back against the hospital bed. She was comforted slightly. "Where's my husband? I don't see him. How long have I been out?" she whispered.

The nurse went to her side. "Well, we've had the pleasure of your company for about six hours." He smiled at her, the kind that shows empathy. "The doctor will be along shortly. Rest for now, and I'll let her know you're awake." He pulled the curtain around the track to cross in front. "You're lucky, Mrs. Stevens." He ducked out toward the station and left her with her thoughts.

There was a hum of excitement in the hall. Curtains were pulled closed and open, scraping along their aluminum tracks. Patients cried out while children whimpered a few beds down. There were no real rooms. It was a city hospital because there were privacy curtains that separated the beds in five-foot sections. Chattering came from all directions. She closed her eyes and took a steadying breath in through her nose out through her mouth.

She coughed. It hurt.

Her throat was raw, and the clean oxygen was cold and forced her awake. She didn't want to sleep. The fluorescent lights seemed to brighten as she took deeper breaths. The coolness made her feel good despite the burning in her nasal passages. It also made her aware.

Aware that her home was gone.

Aware that her husband was not sitting with her in the small space. He should have been where the empty black plastic chair sat.

Her heart quickened. She swayed, dizzy from the deep breathing coupled with fear. *Where is he?* she thought. If she lay in the bed, sore and exhausted, what must he feel? She swallowed back tears. "Nurse? Nurse!"

Sophia knew it was a long shot. Calling out for a nurse in the Emergency Room was a common practice. Most often, it was not emergency related. She realized then, her reason for calling was also not an emergency in the kind that required a nurse. But one that felt like her heart would burst if she couldn't find a knowing body, to ask about other patients or survivors.

She laid back against the bed and watched the drips in her IV, petting Winston, and drifted to sleep.

***

"Mrs. Stevens," a female voice called. "Mrs. Stevens."

The voice urged Sophia awake. She blinked her eyes open. Two uniformed officers were standing at the foot of her gurney with a tall blonde female doctor with her hands in her white lab coat pockets.

"Yes?" she whispered.

"How are you feeling, Mrs. Stevens," the doctor asked. "How is your pain?"

"I...I'm okay," she muttered as she struggled to sit upright on the air mattress, using her elbows and forearms to maneuver to a seated position.

The doctor raised the head on the bed higher. "You have a few burns on your hands, and you took in some smoke, but you'll be alright. We're moving you to your room now. They'll be here to get you shortly."

Sophia nodded.

The doctor exchanged glances with the officers, and the female officer stepped forward.

"Mrs. Stevens, I'm Officer Carillo, and this is Officer Davis."

Sophia closed her eyes and squeezed to slow the flood of tears that knew to come. She folded her lips and held Winston's head. "You're here about my husband, aren't you?"

"We are," Officer Davis said. He held his hat in front of him, his thumb rubbing over the rim.

"He didn't make it out," she sighed, not believing those words crossed her lips.

"No," Officer Carillo sighed. "I'm so sorry."

Sophia leaned back against the pillows. Tears leaked from her swollen eyes. "Thank you."

The officers bowed their heads and ducked out of the privacy curtain, leaving the doctor to stand alone at the foot of the bed. *NO, NO, NO, How could this be happening, why me? Why Jonathon? WHY? What am I going to do?*

"Is there someone I can call? A parent or sibling?"

Sophia searched her mind for names. *Who should I call? Who did I want to call? No one.* She wanted to be left alone. To think; process what happened in the last half a day. She couldn't wrap her head around the realization that she'd had her final moments with her dear husband. She wasn't ready to let him go. Not yet. And not like that, a victim of the wildfires.

Why did the good days seem so far away? In a moment, they seemed like years, although in reality, it was hours. They had laughed and sipped wine over dinner. They were supposed to have coffee this morning. And fresh mango they bought yesterday at the market.

"It's all gone," she said to the doctor. "The mangoes, the coffee, my house."

"I'm really sorry, Sophia."

Sophia looked up. "I-I have a sister in Boise. You can call her." She gave the doctor the number and closed her eyes. "Thank you, doctor."

The young doc ducked out of the curtained room and disappeared into the hustle and bustle beyond.

Sophia turned to her side and let the tears drip over her pillow. Winston laid on the floor beside the bed , head drooped, ears and tail down. He was whimpering, he was looking for Jonathan, but he was also here for Sophia, protecting her. Her sister lived in Idaho. The last thing she wanted was to move into their home with two cats, two kids, and a husband, all tucked into the suburbs. She wanted to be alone.

Chapter 3

DETERMINATION

DETERMINATION

A week had passed. Sophia spent seven long dreary days with her sister. She loved her sister and yet, Sophia wanted to be alone to process, to think, to do nothing. She wanted to disappear into solitary confinement. After losing her bandages, since she only had minor burns, she was capable of living on her own. She had spoken to a wildfire attorney to get everything straight because phone calls to the insurance company were like playing a game of Round Robin while getting things settled with her husband's affairs. He worked for the state and had an insurance policy that would help her rebuild if she so chose. But after endless phone calls and media coverage with constant pictures of homes reduced to bits of rubble, she was done.

"I'm taking a sabbatical," she told her sister. "I'm going off the grid. I want to feel the quiet. I don't want pity or empathy. I had a wonderful life, and I need time to grieve. John and I talked about it. I'm going to do it. I know I can do it. I've prepared for it. Winston and I will be fine."

"How long?" her sister had asked.

"A year, maybe two. I want to get away from all of it... all of this."

Her sister didn't try to stop her. She just stood on her front step and waved as Sophia and Winston drove away in her Jeep CJ5 back to California.

Sophia didn't feel like having a memorial for Jonathan. It was still too fresh, too painful. She knew she wouldn't be able to bear the looks of pity from her and Jonathan's friends, so she decided, for the time being, to carry his urn with her and sprinkle a small bit of his ash when she drove past a place or something that she knew he would have loved. It was as if he was on this journey with her. She could almost feel his breath on her cheek and she was strangely comforted.

***

Sophia arrived at the burned remains of their home. Her face was gaunt with sorrow as she approached the lot where their house once stood. *Nobody can prepare you to see what once was your house and property,* she thought. *Now, just a charred mess of rubble.* The blackened tree trunks and scorched pines tainted the landscape that was once a thriving community. Not a house stood unscathed.

She pulled up to the curb and stepped onto the road. With her list of items to do from CALFIRES, Sophia went in. There were still hot spots that the firefighters told the neighbors to be aware of. The underground network of roots and trees can still be smoldering for weeks. She couldn't help focusing on the frames of twisted metal that arose from the ash-filled foundation. The air was thick with the smell of burnt wood.

She wandered over to where she had last seen Jonathan. He ran into the front door; the back of the house had already been engulfed. She wondered if he was a part of the ashes as she walked through the rubble. Winston tried to pull her to the door, but she tugged back at him. "No, boy, don't go there; there's too much debris." But she couldn't hold him back. He ran to the area which used to be the room where John would sit, and he would lay by his master's feet all day, watching TV together. "This was the living room, the TV was over there, and the fireplace. John's chair." The chair was a pile of springs now. But Winston sniffed it and whined, and he knew. He just sat there and waited. Sophia wondered; *does he know John is never coming back?* She glanced around the room. "The safe! Oh, my Goodness! The safe is still standing. How? The fire was so hot it melted everything surrounding it, but the double-sided steel walls."

Her neighbors used sifters to find some piece of their life, while holding on to hope.

But they have each other, she thought.

She cleared a pile of broken cement and burned boards. She used a charred coffee table leg remnant to free the safe's steel case. It took a good amount of tossing debris and earnest digging, but she got the door free to where she could get it open. She couldn't remember the combination, *L8, R11, L71? Darn, that wasn't it, R8, L11, R71? That didn't work either.* Then she remembered the key; she had the duplicate on the keychain in her pocket from the set she used for the Jeep CJ5. She took the key from her pocket and opened the safe.

Her husband's 12 gage Browning shotgun and his SIG SAUR 1911 semi-automatic, slugs, and scattershot seemed okay. She'd take them to the range where her husband taught her to shoot. It was necessary in the wild. She grabbed the adapters that could be used to shoot any size bullet in the 12 gauge! Wow, John was such a planner. She remembered thinking that gadget was a piece of junk but now she knew he was brilliant! Any type of ammo could be used in the 12 gauge shotgun with those adapters, great for living off the grid.

A few folders with their marriage license and framed wedding day picture were wrapped in a fire-retardant blanket, the one she couldn't find. She carried the contents to the car in a garbage bag, intent on going over them in the privacy of her hotel room.

She went back to the safe and opened the small door within. Sophia expected to find John's pistol for work. Instead, she found Jonathan's prized orange pocketknife. The signed pocketknife from Dick Proenneke, the man that survived 30 years all alone in Alaska, built his cabin at Lake Clark National Park and Preserve with his bare hands. He'd lived there until his 80's when he moved back to California.

She remembered when they were on a hike to Yosemite. She and John were climbing Nevada falls and waiting for the next tram down to the valley floor when they spotted him. John was overjoyed by it. Proenneke was a survivalist. A man who Jonathan wanted to become, his "role model." He was thankful for all and wasted nothing. Proenneke utilized every piece of meat, carcass, leather, and hoof of his hunt. John did the same. And they both treasured life, all walks of life. They were men who celebrated life.

Sophia stuck the knife in her hoodie pocket. There was a piece of leather tied with rawhide tucked beside an envelope behind the knife. "What's this?" Sophia opened the leather scroll. "A map? On a piece of leather?" She studied the markings, but the only clear thing was a large black *X*. Her heart pounded. "Has John been keeping a secret from me all these years?" She turned the leather over, but only one side had markings. "What does this mean? Why?" Her fingers shook; her body trembled. Unfolding the letter, she recognized the familiar writing.

Dear Sophie,

If you are reading this letter, I love you, and I know you have found it for a reason. All these years, I have been going back to the cabin and adding things to this Survival list. I know I have been teaching you how to get along without me, and I know you can do it. I have been planning for a long time. So please go there as we planned. Since we started going there every year, I have been adding to my collection. I have left this map with directions to the buried treasure.

When you get to the cabin, go to the fireplace, find the red brick. It will be loose. That is your first clue. Remember, I love you. And when you follow my directions, you will understand that

X Marks The Spot

Never Give Up, Keep on Going

Yours always,
Love, John

PS

Sophia, your first thing to do is remember to prepare:
Locate Food, water, shelter; secure your perimeter.

Supplies For Survival:

Familiarize yourself with your surroundings.
Firestarter
Straw/Water purifier
First aid kit

***

Winston jerked the leash, pulling toward where the garage had been. The bronco's red trim was now reduced to a lake of melted metal. Orange and white twisted plastic was all that remained of their motorcycles. Sophia jerked along with him, and the knife bounced from her pocket.

"Oh, come on," Sophia blurted. The knife fell into the debris. She worked at clearing the rest of the debris around safe and was relieved when she could pluck the orange knife from the pile of ash. Tears wet her lashes. "I got it."

She was meant to find it. Was it a sign from her beloved husband? She was certain the knife was the last piece of her life with him. It connected them on an emotional level. The joy, grief, and acceptance he felt then faced her now. She took it to the car. The lawyer already had crews scheduled for cleanup and construction, though over six months out. Search and Rescue teams had already scoured the neighborhood for survivors and remains. Life and Death. How odd, life goes on after death. Nothing left in the rubble could mean more than the knife, the letter, and her marriage license. One would go in a safe deposit box, the other carried close to her heart.

Sophia clutched the knife and hugged it to her chest. It was a piece of her husband. His hands had touched it, and it was now a sense of his touch against her own. She swore she could feel his warmth on the cool blade.

"What am I doing here?" she asked herself.

It was clear that she had no plan. She was without her soulmate, her counterpart. They traveled and explored, trekked, and camped. But all they did, was as a couple. *Who is Sophia Stevens?* she thought. *What do I like? How do I move forward? How can I do this on my own?* She always promised him that if he were to leave their life together first, she would carry on no matter what happened. She would live her life to the fullest.

She pressed the knife to her cheek and tucked it in her hoodie pocket. It hung loosely over her black leggings. A couple wandered down the street, stepping over debris in the unrecognizable road. They paused in front of Sophia, arm in arm. They exchanged a weak smile and waved at her. She didn't return the smile but waved. She squeezed the knife in her pocket and sighed. All around, there were charred trees, silent from birds that fled and remained too distant to fill the hills with their song.

Blackened studs stood where thick walls and living rooms should have been. Melted televisions, contorted stoves, and lone fireplaces dotted the lots surrounding her ghost of a home. An ATV wound its way up the hill and past her house, weaving through lawns around pools littered with bricks. Electric lines dangled from mangled meters. Charred appliances were strewn about. It sickened her. But it also sparked her ambition.

She took the knife from her pocket and whispered, "One last adventure, Babe. X marks the spot."

Chapter 4

UNFORGETTABLE

The sunrise gleamed pink and lavender over the mountains. The low green grasses glistened with morning dew, and the trees offered a soft red glow to the path toward Sophia's new destination—a lakeside cabin on a parcel in Idaho. In exchange for an uninterrupted stay, her aunt-in-law, Margie, asked for matching satellite phones to stay in touch, so everyone knew she was safe. It was supposed to be the future home for Sophia and John. They hoped to live off-grid there, a dream John had from his early youth. Aunt Margie was now 75 and ready to retire. As a local from Idaho, she offered to drive up and meet Sophia on occasion. But this was Sophia's journey. One she had to make alone. To find her purpose, a mission of self-discovery. Margie understood.

Sophia considered trading in her vintage Jeep CJ5 or leaving it at her sister's place for a more modern (some say reliable) Land Rover but she realized that the CJ5 was basic, no electric gadgets, an "essentials only" simple vehicle, when dealing with the unknown. It was the better choice. She did not need potential electrical problems when she had a reliable durable vehicle at her fingertips. It was perfect for the rugged terrain she hoped to encounter to bring back those familiar thrills she used to enjoy.

Along with her list of survival items, she knew a repair list was necessary. She wrote down John's go-to tools and ventured to Home Depot with Winston in tow. Sophia knew that she would need a saw, pliers, chainsaw, a hammer, a screwdriver, nails, and screws. She opted for the all-in-one tool kit, some Superglue and zip ties. Her usual routine would be to triple-check her husband's list of essentials before every camping excursion. She doubted she would need much more as they had been to the cabin on a year-by-year basis. She left with a single bag. The Jeep was tight when packed, and she needed all the room she could save for her last stop, the Country Store.

She took the knife from her pocket and set it on the seat next to the orange Home Depot bag. "I miss you, Babe," she said to the knife. It had been a very long week without him, but the letter kept her moving forward in her journey— that and Winston, who had become her guardian.

***

Another stop to REI (Recreational Equipment) for more of the list: a basic sewing kit, extra thread, a magnesium fire starter, two tarps, a pillow, a camping chair, machete, mess kit, folding knife, duct tape, glow sticks, candles, batteries, ammo, an astronaut blanket, iodine tablets, and a fully stocked first aid kit complete with butterflies.

The irony of going off-grid and needing supplies before doing so was not lost on Sophia. During her research, she discovered many ways to go off-grid and learned that, in a nutshell, it meant living without electricity. She could have her supplies and make minimal trips to civilization if she chose. It was a choice she made to restart.

To restart her life, her goals, and all that popped up in between was going to take time. It would take time to let go of her husband and their adventures. Going to their parcel of wilderness would give her that needed time to reflect and learn.

✳✳✳

She grabbed two arctic sleeping bags. She figured two would give her a way to bundle up for warmth, and a second bag was good to have on hand in the event one got wet. The downside of going to a place you've never stayed alone was that you had to remember everything you needed. Since she and her husband had spent a fair amount of time in REI, she knew she could get in and out.

She left the store wheeling the cart to her Jeep. When she opened the back, it looked like she was moving. *I guess restarting and moving are similar enough,* she thought. The back was overstuffed with bags of supplies. She shoved the sleeping bags in the backseat and closed the door.

It appeared to be a lot of stuff, but she knew supplies dwindled faster than she expected from her time RVing. She knew there would be a quaint store at some juncture where she could grab some jerky, dried milk, and oats. The idea of going off-grid hadn't meant that she would become a homesteader yet. She hadn't brought seeds or starter chickens. That was not in her immediate future. Instead, she would make an occasional trip for dry goods and whatever she saw a need for. But there would be no electricity and no people.

She double-checked the tires and patted the hood.

***

Sophia pulled into the dirt parking lot of a time-loved store a good 100 miles over the northern Idaho border and went inside pushing a paint-chipped shopping cart. There were bait buckets and fishing poles covered with dust along the front wall. She grabbed one of each and a small, stocked tackle box with lures, hooks, sinkers, and a bobber. She figured there would be plenty of bait around but opted to include a small straining net from the wall. At least she could catch crayfish and minnows if the need arose. *Worms should be plentiful*, she thought.

She gathered an ample supply of potatoes, jerky, flour, rice, and oats. In doing so, she saw a hand-written sign above cases of canned goods:

Survivalist Special

There were stacks of canned tomatoes, beans, green beans, carrots, peas, and corn. She grabbed one of each. A case had twelve cans. If she rationed, there would be a good three months of food. Of course, edible plants and wildlife would stretch that.

As she pushed her loaded cart around the last aisle, she passed the coffee and tea section. There was a box of assorted herbal teas. She added three to the cart. Tea was part of her nighttime routine her whole life. She couldn't remember a time when she didn't have tea. Even as young as one, she had chamomile. It soothed and warmed the soul.

She rounded the corner and went to the counter, where a young man squatted by the register stocking candy and snacks.

Why not, she thought as she chose an assortment of chocolate bars, a container of nuts, a bottle each of Zinfandel and Pinot Noir. *I'm out here to live, not suffer.* She smiled to herself.

The clerk rose from his stooping, chewing gum popping. It was clear he didn't want to be there, and she had inconvenienced him. But that didn't matter to Sophia. She put a grin on her face and greeted him. After all, he might be the last human being she ever saw. "Hi, Sophia Stevens." She extended her hand.

He blinked at her. "Tom." It took a few moments, but he grabbed her hand and shook it. "Where you from?" he asked. His eyes focused on her tan Danner boots with red laces.

"You heard of the wildfires, I suppose." She pulled the orange knife from her hoodie pocket. "Tom, this is what's left of my husband. I am out here to learn whatever life has to teach me. I know I don't look the part, but we loved camping and the outdoors. This is my way of saying 'Good-bye' and 'Hello' all at the same time."

Tom swallowed. "I'm sorry."

Sophia shrugged. "Thanks. I hear that a lot. When I was on the opposite side of the conversation, I said the same thing. It sucks because it's uncomfortable. You can forget my story. That you ever heard me say it." She put the tackle box on the conveyor belt and put out her hand. "Hi, I'm Sophia Stevens. What's your name?"

Tom took her hand and smiled, weak and questioning. "Tom."

"Nice to meet you, Tom."

"Likewise," the young man said.

He scanned her supplies and stacked them in cloth bags. When he was done, he stretched over to look in the shopping cart. "You'll need a can opener and a wine opener."

"Oh, I knew I'd miss something."

Tom grabbed the manual openers from a display by the front register. "A lot of folks overlook them. We just started keeping them handy."

"Well, thank you, Tom. It would be a hard night trying to work those cans loose with a screwdriver."

They laughed the uncomfortable laugh that strangers exchanged when they knew the situation wasn't funny but rather a matter of empathy and acknowledged pity. He loaded the bags in the cart on top of the cases of cans. "Hope we see you back soon, Ms. Sophia."

She smiled a genuine smile. The kind that one gives when they are caught off guard. "Thank you, Tom. You just might."

On her way out, an older woman in an oversized red flannel jacket and jeans reached for Sophia's arm. "Excuse me. Did you say your name is Sophia Stevens?"

"I did," Sophia confirmed.

"I'm the owner of this store and knew your husband, Mrs. Stevens. He left an envelope with me a while back. It was a just in case." Her eyes twinkled with relatable tears. "His aunt told me about his passing." She reached in her pocket and handed Sophia a folded envelope. "If you need anything, I'll find it for you."

Sophia took the envelope. "Thank you, ma'am." She hurried her cart to the Jeep, eager to read what Jonathan had left her.

Sophia managed to get all her purchases in the vehicle and returned the cart before opening the envelope. She wanted no distractions to her husband's words.

Sophia,

By now, you have been hard at work: planning and remembering. Most likely, you have not ventured to the cabin yet, and this was your last stop. Here is a list of everything to take with you for this first night. Remember, I love you.

X marks the spot

Jonathan

Survival List:

1. A solar charger
2. Astronaut blanket
3. Mirror, whistle, compass
4. First Aid kit with Butterflies
5. Can opener, canned food
6. Soap/toilet paper
7. Water purification supplies, i.e., LifeStraw, ceramic/UV water treatment, or iodine tablets
8. A pole, hooks, lures, and sinkers for fishing.
9. Gun
10. Ammo, any size will fit the 12 gauge with adapters
11. A knife, machete

12. Duct tape
13. Flares
14. Glow sticks
15. Fuel

Repair List:

16. Shovel
17. Hammer, wrench, pliers
18. Nails, screws
19. Screwdrivers, reg and phillip's
20. Zip ties
21. Saw
22. Pencil
23. Manual air pump
24. Axe
25. Leather work gloves

Living Without Electricity List:

26. Hand sanitizer and Vaseline (doubles as a firestarter)
27. Candles and flashlight
28. Cotton balls
29. Batteries
30. Gas
31. Generator
32. Solar water heater kit
33. Laundry hand washer
34. Manual chain saw with hand straps
35. Solar summer shower

Love,
John

Sophia was pleased that she had everything on his list. She already had flares in the back of the Jeep as a standard practice. She wondered if he would be proud of her. *Wow, it seems like ages ago. I took it for granted. He was always the one who took care of things. Did I remember it all? Now is the test,* she thought, and then took out the knife and looked up to the sky. "Jonathan, if you're looking down, I hope you're proud of me."

Chapter 5

TANGERINE SKIES

Sophia followed the asphalt road up an incline that offered breathtaking views of blue-gray mountains and disappeared into the periwinkle sky. It was the kind of vision that was specific to northern Idaho, the Coeur d'Alene Mountains.

The spiked peaks soared in the distance. According to her research, there were numerous lakes and streams in the area. Their land, in particular, had a large lake. It reminded her of when she was a young girl, and her parents took her to Lake Tahoe on one of their family vacations. She remembered sitting on the shore, fascinated by the glass-like surface that reflected the tangerine hues. An unforgettable sunset where her mother brought her tea before taking a seat on the stones beside her. The lake house was a mere thousand feet from shore. They sat, sharing the chill that came with the celestial display's appearance. And even then, they did not leave until her father called from the deck. He'd started the tabletop firepit for s'mores.

Sophia glanced at the knife she had nestled in a towel on the front seat of the Jeep CJ5. "It's been a long time since I thought about those days." She turned off the main road onto a dirt pass that led to their parcel. As she drove, she remembered Jonathan pointing out all the different trees native to Idaho. She listed the ones she could remember to the knife beside her and Winston, who was asleep on the floor beneath it. "There was the Red Fir also called the Douglas Fir, the White Fir called the Grand Fir, and there were lots of Mountain Hemlocks. Oh, and I passed the Lodgepole Pines with the bare trunks a while ago." She ducked low to glimpse the trees as they descended the mountain. "Oh, those are Engelmann Spruces and Ponderosa Pines. I'll keep looking for the Pacific Yew and Subalpine Firs."

Sophia drove through the towering mix of pines and firs that loomed over the pass, blocking the sun in parts.

It was hit or miss with overhanging trees, a rocky stream that wore a trench through what she assumed was the old ingress. It wasn't anything concerning as she was used to rough terrain on her camping adventures with her husband.

She continued over a few rocks and downed limbs. Drove over a log too large to move but rotted enough to crumble as she passed over. The pass turned into a leveled-out grassland. The tall yellow-green flora swayed in the breeze. She drove through heart fluttering and focused on a grey roof that emerged from the distance. *That's it,* she thought. Although filled with excitement, she kept her slow progression. Experience taught her obstacles like to appear when you let your guard down. The last thing she needed was to get stranded, unable to drive.

"Two hours from the store to the pass turn off, then another fifty to maneuver the terrain. We don't want to have to hike our way home," she commented to the knife. "But if we need to, I'm prepared with my backpack." Sophia knew that John made sure all the vehicles had an emergency backpack that was always ready with a camel pack of water, Power Bar for emergency energy, solar charger, crank radio, a mirror, glow stick, batteries, small flashlight, power gummies, a stick of chewing gum for chewing and for an emergency "glue", hiking boots, a hat, sunglasses, sunscreen, insect repellent, a whistle, magnesium fire starter, and a smaller first aid kit.

∗∗∗

The far side of the lake glistened in the distance; its shores hidden by towering trees. Driving closer, the little red cabin on the edge of the lake emerged. There was a dock off the porch and an outhouse near the back. A stack of wood poked out from under a tarp beside the facing wall.

She kept her speed, even though she wanted to get in there—to see the familiar, quaint abode that was to become her new home. There was a fiberglass rowboat upside down and tied to the dock, now shrouded with overgrown ferns. She remembered John once told her that Northern Idaho had one of the highest diversities of ferns. She loved how they covered the land between the two buildings. Tall grasses seemed to only grow on one side of the road. She pulled up to the porch and put the Jeep in park next to wild strawberry and fireweed plants.

✳✳✳

"Remember," John had said, crouching beside the lake, "edible plants in the wilderness are the difference between life and death. Idaho is home to tasty wild edibles, such as morels, huckleberries, hawthorn fruits, and cattail roots. But also fireweed, which is high in vitamin C and wild strawberries. But never guess. If you don't know, let it go. It's better not to eat something you can't properly identify."

He plucked a few flowers from a serviceberry stem and handed them to her. "These have been used in Native medicinal practices for centuries."

They hiked over the mountain that day. Sophia learned about the fresh earthy taste of roots and the refreshing leaves of the Field Mint.

∗∗∗

Sophia sighed and hopped out of the Jeep. Winston was already ahead of her, sweeping the grounds around the cabin. She found the key to the cabin on the set for the Jeep.

∗∗∗

The wooden structure stood solid but worn. The roof was shingled with shale, and a coat of red paint peeled from the rough-hewn boards. Sophia approached the cabin, taking the time to appreciate each hand-cut board. There were knots and cracks. Jonathon and she had vacationed here. His presence here in the past made the present soothing to Sophia as she pictured him when they stayed here before. It calmed the turmoil she was leaving behind.

Sophia stepped onto the little porch. Its overhang was enough to keep the rain off the entrance. She unlocked the door, took the knife from her hoodie pocket, and stepped over the wooden threshold.

Chapter 6
A NEW BEGINNING

Sophia expected to find the cabin needing a good dose of TLC. But upon entry, it was just the opposite. The walls were planked with rough-cut wood, the cast iron potbelly stove was ready for use, and on the left side of the stone fireplace was red, painted brick. It was a one-room cabin, so the bed was a full-sized mattress on a hand-carved wooden frame. In the corner was a rocking chair next to a bookshelf. There were novels and paper for journaling, but no journals. She wondered if John had hidden some in the cabin.

The windows were dusty but intact. The forest green curtains hung right where she last saw them. There was a fireplace tool set with a small broom by the stove. She spotted a bucket beneath the sink and grabbed it. The four-foot countertop needed a good scrubbing.

She took the bucket to the lake and brought it back, collecting small sticks along her way. "May as well get a fire going before I find my clue," she said to the knife. "I'll gather as much wood as I can carry every time I go out. I'll grab a sleeping bag and the food before I come in and settle." She patted the knife in her pocket. "Oh, and I'm going to call you Jack."

***

Before wetting the dust-laden surfaces, she decided to use the broom to gather any loose dirt. She also didn't see any other vessel to carry water, so she decided against putting the dirty rags in the bucket. She was going to need that.

The stove looked to be in good shape, but she was sure there would be some critter nest in the stove pipe. She tapped it with the broom handle. Nothing. She decided to look in the chimney and the outside of the pipe. She knew she should clear them from debris before attempting to start a fire.

"It's been at least a year since they've been lit," she said.

There was a metal toolbox behind the stove. Sophia opened it in hopes of finding something to help her with the process. She was delighted to find a wire brush already used to scrape the creosote from the chimneys. There was also a canvas bag which John used to collect soot and debris, and a bottle of distilled vinegar.

Of all the things she bought at the store, a bucket wasn't one of them. She searched the leaves around the cabin for any hidden gems but fell short. But there were some larger tools: a homemade ladder, ax, shovel, and rake wrapped in a frayed tarp. She went to the outhouse and found a smaller bucket. It looked clean enough to scrub the chimneys, so she added a bit of vinegar in the smaller container before adding water. Since it was early September, she knew she'd need a fire pronto even if curiosity were peeking at every turn. She eyed the red brick.

She placed the ladder against the shale-shingled overhang. "Wow, John sure kept up the place," she said. The roof was intact. Flashing was secure around each chimney. Since the slope wasn't so steep that she couldn't stand, she went back down to the Jeep and grabbed the rope tie that she used to keep the supplies in place. It was the plastic kind Home Depot provided to contractors and customers for tying down their goods. She was glad to have used some to secure the loose supplies. Since there was a sturdy, slim tree next to the cabin, she put the ladder on that side so she could tie the rope to the tree and then thread it through the belt loops in the waist of her Northface cargo pants.

Cargo pants were her go-to when camping because of the extra pockets. There was room for fire starters and lures. Now she was glad because of the belt loops. *Maybe not the strongest security measure, but it's what I've got,* she thought. She had a large carabiner and a rock-climbing sling as well. She used a smaller piece of twine rope to secure the ladder making a square knot as John had taught her, one that was from his search and rescue training. When satisfied, she went up on the roof.

The chimneys had wire mesh over the tops. "Awesome," she whispered. She removed each cap and ran the broom handle and wire brush down before securing them back in place.

***

Back inside the cabin, Sophia took out her mess kit, magnesium fire starter, and sticks she had gathered. She brought in the quarter cord of wood she bought and stacked it by the door. Next, she started a fire with a few sticks on a cut of wood using a trick John taught her. She put a drop of hand sanitizer on a cotton ball and the sticks to make the fire. She poured a bit of water into the mess kit pot. It was a small pot but big enough to pour into the metal cup for tea.

Winston had followed her in and took his place by the rocking chair. With the fire going and water heating, Sophia felt settled for the evening. She went to the red brick and wiggled it from its place. Another letter rolled as a scroll fell from the hole.

Sophia,

I know you secured your shelter and have a fire. You started water and have food. Now, get a good night's sleep, and in the morning, before the sun hits the nine o'clock shadow, follow the ridge to the right side of the cabin. As you look out, you will follow the path along the Huckleberry bushes to find a stream, lined with cattail roots. There you will see a mountain, a single peak. It is the one I took you to every year. Take your 12-gauge and find the tree with a hollow where lightning struck. Walk ten paces away from the stalk and turn to your left 90 degrees, and you will find yourself looking at a flat mesa. Shoulder your gun and point it to the West. Now aim for the only treetop and shoot. You can't miss it. With any luck, it will split into two distinct parts. Follow the left branch, and it will take you through a maze of Hawthorn

fruit trees. Remember?
I love you,
John

The thought of going on a scavenger hunt created by John excited her. After starting her tea, she set out to wipe down the wooden countertop and sink basin. There were cabinets with critter leavings that she decided to use the vinegar for and set off for bringing in the rest of the supplies. The sun was low and light fading. Among the treasures in the toolbox, she found a wind-up flashlight. She used it to bring in the dry goods and a case of water. "Well, Jack. I think that's enough for today," she said to the knife that was now placed on a nest of fabric she had fashioned on the rocker.

Sophia fastened the two iron latches on the door and spread one of the sleeping bags on the mattress. She put the bucket of lake water in the sink and set out making plans for the coming days as she nibbled a bit of beef jerky and sipped her tea. It was a long way from being home, but in time it would be hers—theirs.

***

"Sophia, come on. You've got to see these Hawthorn Fruit Trees. There are like twenty of them," John called to Sophia, who was catching up after getting her shoelace caught on an exposed root. She had to retie it and tuck it in.

"This is beautiful, John," She exclaimed when she got there. "Can we eat these?"

"Yep, and their medicinal. The land is full of rewards. Look at that peak from here," he said, pointing to a distant mountain. It seemed to rise alone. "I love this place, Sophe."

Sophia hugged into his arm. "Me too, John."

"This is a good place to find rabbits. Especially in winter. I bet the low-lying brush brings them in." He kissed her cheek. "Let's not forget this place. You never know when we'll need it."

★★★

Sophia changed into a pair of sweatpants and a sweatshirt; nestled into the rocking chair beside Jack, she drifted to sleep dreaming about the real Jonathan and the last time they went camping. In her dreams, she allowed herself to cry.

Chapter 7

SERENITY

The morning sun burst through the window in orange beams. The light struck where Sophia's head stuck out of the sleeping bag. It was nature's alarm clock. She blinked her eyes open, her heart warmed by the golden glow of the wooded cabin space. The natural yellows absorbed the sun's rays. She slid from the bed to start the stove for coffee and opted to make extra water for oatmeal and honey. It seemed like a nice day to start with a bit of sweetness.

After lighting the fire, she opened the door. The lake stretched before her, its surface glass-like and reflecting the sunrise on the calm waters as it had been all those years back, on Lake Tahoe.

She went back in and poured water into her little pot. She pulled the rocking chair to the porch-like entryway. By the time she was done, the water was hot. She put a few grains of instant coffee in the cup and poured the boiling water over them, swirling until it was dissolved. Focused on the scene before her, she settled in the rocker and sipped.

The crisp morning air carried the scent of evergreens and dew. It was earthy, woody, and all things nature.

Sophia exhaled, a long-awaited expulsion of grief and chaos. It left her in waves as the water's surface held her captive by the genuine magic of all that just is. She closed her eyes and breathed in, counting to five. She let her breath out slower and sipped the coffee. Perhaps because she was starting anew, or because of the moment, she would find peace. Contentment too would come, in time.

A flock of geese skidded over the mid-point of the lake, breaking the mirror. She settled back and took in the coffee's aroma before taking a larger swallow. Without realizing it, she started to rock, a slow, steady rhythm. Her sock-covered toes pushed off the worn boards.

***

"Where do you see us in thirty years?" Sophia asked Jonathan.

He smiled, "Retired. Living in a cabin by a lake."

"Sounds quiet."

"Secluded," he said, then added another log to the fire.

They were camping in Arches National Park. The red stone dulled in the night while the cosmic display overhead took over the endless display of beauty.

"This is breathtaking," Sophia exclaimed.

"There's no light pollution out here. Imagine living like this."

"Mmmm," she said, sipping her tea. "It would be heaven."

They sat back in their canvas camping chairs, staring at the sky.

"We could, you know." Jonathan interrupted the silence.

Sophia looked at him then. "What?"

He crossed his ankles and looked her in the eye. "Go off-grid."

She settled back and sipped again. "You're serious."

"Hell, yeah, I'm serious. Think about it. You, me, living by a lake. Solar power, growing food for more than a windowsill garden, and more fish than we could eat. Wouldn't you like to wake up free? Free from all the rat race and noise?"

Sophia laughed, an excited laugh. It hinted at intrigue and acceptance. "And I suppose you have the perfect place for our new life."

Jonathan poked the fire with the metal poker. "Aunt Maggie's old place. She doesn't use it, Sophe; she'll probably sell it to us just to make sure someone kept it up. My family loved that place. I want to go there more than just once a year."

"Wait, you're talking about moving to Idaho. The Coeur d'Alene Mountains."

"Yup, think about it."

"I will," Sophia smiled and shook her head. "It would be awesome."

"You do remember. It's on a lake."

She laughed, more pronounced. "You know the way to a girl's heart, Jonathan Stevens."

Jonathan laughed in triumph. It was the last time they had camped before he lost his life in the 2017 wildfires. But it wasn't the last they spoke on it. It was a dream they planned to bring to fruition. One that involved the two of them working side by side to reduce their carbon footprint, aid the environment, and live surrounded by the best nature had to offer.

They had gone there every year for the past 15 years, for a week on their vacation, always dreaming of this. And the last five preparing for their escape from reality. From the grid. Never had she imagined that Jonathon was so methodical. Never had she thought when she woke up in the mornings, and he was gone early, or just sneaking back from a hike, that he was slowly creating their getaway. Wow, if she could only trace his steps and hope she could understand the map she found in the rubble, inside the safe.

✱✱✱

Sophia sipped her coffee, brought back to the present by the sound of a hawk calling overhead. It glided over the treetops and circled back around the cabin. She blinked her eyes to clear the daydreams, making her mind clear for the day ahead.

The geese flapped their wings, breaking the water's surface. Rings and ripples ebbed from where they landed. A single smaller ring appeared closer toward Sophia and the dock. *Was it a fish, turtle, beaver from below?* A fish jumped not far from what had caught her attention, *a small school.* She would have food when it was necessary.

The ripples subsided, and the smooth surface extended to an area sprinkled with decaying trunks and cattails. Lily pads littered the water a good way in. She looked around at the carpet of pine needles, yellowed and compressed.

There were hollows at the bottoms of a few trees that lined the lake closest to her. She wondered if there were newts or furred critters living in them. A glance at the treetops told her there were squirrels. The large nests were nestled into the tops of what she identified as a maple. "I can tap that," she said. "Maple water." She remembered Jonathan telling her about the magic of trees.

***

"You ever had maple water before it's been boiled to sap, Sophe?"

"Can't say I have."

"It's good. Of course, it's safer to boil it, but if you ever find yourself alone, know that with a good knife, a stick, and something to catch the sap, you'll have more than 24 antioxidants, manganese, potassium, and a slew of vitamins and minerals."

"And how would I know if it was a maple?"

"The leaves look like your hand, 5 points. But you can drink from the walnut, birch, and hickory trees also. You can make pine needle tea for vitamin "C" too. Just throw fresh pine needles in water and boil."

Sophia hugged into him. They were camping in Yellowstone. "You don't have to worry about me. I'll have you, and you can take care of it."

"And if I'm not around?" He looked down at her, eyes steady on hers.

"Then I keep exploring all the wonders mother nature has to offer for the both of us." She smiled, but her eyes did not hold the spark necessary to make him believe her words.

"Promise me, Babe. You won't stop living if I go first. We both know my job as a ranger puts me at risk."

Sophia knew what it entailed, but she didn't want to accept it. "I promise."

***

Sophia took Jack from her pocket. "I kept my promise, Jack." She sipped her coffee and watched the geese flap in the water and dive, tails up. The tightness she'd had in her chest since Jonathan's passing lifted. The serenity of the water and animals going about their day distracted her from the outside—her old reality.

A red squirrel darted in front of her and danced its way up the maple tree. It peeked around the trunk at her. She sat still as they made eye contact. The squirrel scampered up the tree stopping every few feet to check on her. It reached a branch midway up and took its station, keeping watch over Sophia.

She waved at the critter. "Hey, I'm a friend."

The squirrel sat on the branch staring at Winston as he scampered back to Sophia's side.

Sophia shook her head. "We'll leave you to your chores. Speaking of, I have to get on some of my own." It was then she realized she had to ready her own nest.

Sophia needed the outhouse, but it was something she avoided. The outside needed very little repair. The white paint was peeling off the old wood planks, but that was the extent of the disrepair. She took the broom with her. Upon opening the door, she started waving the broom in the air to collect any webs and spider carcasses. She continued to the seated area and floor, surprised there was a composting toilet. "John, got a real toilet!" Once she was satisfied that any unwanted critters wouldn't be invading her time, she put the broom outside and did her business. The last time she was there, it was a true outhouse with a hole in the ground.

From the inside, the building was more than satisfactory. Besides the composting toilet, the walls were lined with wooden planks, and a metal army locker stood in the corner. Upon opening the locker, she found a water purification system, a folding shovel, rope, spray paint, field guides to tracking, edible plants, a HAM radio, an N95 mask, goggles, earplugs, and a bag of kitty litter. Sophia got the suspicion that John was all ready for going off-grid. With that in mind, she decided to tackle her gear lists.

One obstacle abolished; the sewage system is a go. It was a big part of living off the grid by law. Besides food, there were three main requirements.

1. You must have an energy source.

2. A sewage collection system had to be in place.

3. A water system had to be accessible.

Sophia had written the list in her phone.

***

It was a good day to start as the skies were clear, with a light breeze that blew now and then. She took the last swallow of the now bitter cold coffee she'd left on the porch and went back into the little red cabin. "Today is the day to pack up my lists of gear and supplies and find the X on the map." She took the piece of leather from her pocket and unfolded it. There, in the center, was a red square. "That must be the cabin." A large black X was in front of the square. There was a compass rose, but it didn't make sense. She had to follow John's clues.

She gathered her packs and dumped the contents onto the bed to ensure she had all she needed. She grabbed the inventory list for her gear bag: HAM radio, solar hand crank radio, shovel, hand strap-chain saw, spray paint, wire, duct tape, face goggles, N95 mask, ear plugs, super glue for minor cuts and repairs, mini first-aid kit, trail mix, Power Bar, gum for bait. The mini booklets on types of edible plants and animal tracking, an area map, pack of salt, pepper, and sugar, garlic and Ziploc bag,(to get the fleas out of animal fur) She grabbed the folding fishing pole, hooks, mini net, weights, fold up pail, and the Bug-out Backpack with the whistle, mirror, Gatorade powder, filled her camel pack with water and the magnesium fire starter. She had her glow stick, LifeStraw, gloves, a scarf, her hat, an astronaut blanket, ammo, and the 12-gauge shotgun. She also packed a pocket journal and pen. Sophia was ready.

***

It was 8:30 in the morning. John's note said to set out before 9. She had to follow the ridge to the right of the cabin. She promised Winston she would return, but he wouldn't take no for an answer. He whimpered until she gave in. He would not leave her side, he was her guardian. *Okay, let's go Winston.* Sophia closed the door, and stepped off the porch making the right between the cabin and outhouse. It headed into the woods to the path of Huckleberry bushes, a gentle incline around the lake. She came to the spot where the mountain stream flowed into the lake. There was a thick patch of cattails all along the point of their meeting. She took out the note and map. There was a single cattail on the lake's edge, and to the west was a purple mark. "That must be the mountain." The note said to look for a single mountain peak. She glanced toward the opposite side of the lake. Sure enough, there was the tip of a distant mountain peak showing through the trees. She remembered John had pointed it out.

They had hiked around the lake and up the mountain for several days. He took her along the stream to find where smaller streams fed into the one that led to their lake. "Everything is connected," he had said. They stopped to enjoy the view when he stood behind her and pointed in at the purple peak in the distance. "One day, we will hike there. It's another part of the Coeur d'Alene."

Sophia smiled at the memory. She could feel John's arms around her, pointing her in the direction. She put the map back in her pocket and checked the note for the next steps. "I have to find a tree where lightning struck." She studied the tops of the trees. They had grown since they had been there. But to the east, she found the tree. Its black mark healed with new bark; the scarring was still visible. She walked ten paces away to her West, then turned left 90 degrees and walked until she reached the flat mesa, the one where they always planned to make camp. But she wasn't there to set up; she was there to find the X and John's buried treasure. She raised the 12-gauge shotgun, loaded the chamber, and aimed West. When she had the only treetop in her sites, she steadied on a weak point and pulled the trigger.

"You were right. I didn't miss," she said, her face to the sky. The tree had split in two. She followed the left branch, and it did indeed take her to the maze of Hawthorn fruit trees. She wandered her way into them, weaving and searching. There was no X.

Dismayed, Sophia sat on the ground, intent on pulling the map from her pocket, but a rustling noise behind her drew her attention. A low whining growl came from behind a cluster of Hawthorns.

Sophia shouldered the gun and fired over the tree to scare off the predator. She grabbed the orange knife in her pocket and removed it from its sheath. "I think it's a bobcat, Jack. I don't want to kill it." She held the knife in front of her and stepped toward the trees. Winston growled back. He was on guard to protect Sophia. His body stood in alert mode. His head and tail stood at attention. Something was tracking them. Following 6 feet behind in the shadows. Good thing Winston came to protect her.

There was no noise.

"Get out of here," she yelled.

Again, nothing. Then she saw the bobcat, it was in the shadows. He was circling his prey now...drool dripping from his mouth. Winston charged at the cat, It was 50 lbs about the same size as Winston, but its teeth looked sharper and longer. It was hungry. The cat just stood there fangs and claws out, then pounced toward Winston.

"Winston, stop. Come back boy." Sophia had her gun in one hand and her knife in the other. There was a reflection of the Orange knife in the bobcat's eyes, and then like magic, both animals, one domestic and one wild exchanged silent words Looked at one another and sat down as if they were at a peace conference.

This gave Sophia a chance to change her strategy, Calmly she started talking to the wild beast. "Okay, cat, don't be afraid, I won't hurt you. I come in peace. We can all live together in harmony; I am here as a friend. I am here to look for the X. I am here to live off the land like you."

The cat tilted its head to the side, as if he understood, turned around and scampered away. Success! She learned how to connect with animals from Johnathon, but this was her first time that she tried it. Thank Goodness she paid attention. Winston knew as well, his body relaxed.

She put the knife back in its sheath and then in her pocket. "I think he left Jack. Good teamwork, Winston."

She continued searching the trees and came out on the other side of the cluster. There were Ponderosa Pines and a bed of thick needles covering the ground. The mountain crest was ahead. She kept scanning the landscape for an X but did not see anything resembling one. As she walked, she listened for the bobcat with the gun held in front of her. . She knew it was out there, but she was not afraid any longer, she had made a friend.

***

Sophia had been walking for hours. She started with the sun low in the sky, and it was now nearing the western horizon. She looked for the Hawthorn trees but did not see them. She had stopped a few times to snack on her trail mix and sip her Gatorade. She had also started marking the trees she passed with spray paint to know where she had been. The first mark had been where she first merged into the ponderosas. She was going in circles. It was getting late, she had to stop soon, but she would not go home until she found it. She was close, she could feel it and knew she could survive out in the wilderness. She was surrounded by love from Winston, from Jack and from Jonathon.

She patted the knife in her pocket. "Well, Jack. I guess we get to camp here for tonight." She took her shovel and cleared a spot to dig a shallow hollow. She used thin toothpick-sized sticks to make a pile. In the center, she placed a cotton ball and then formed a teepee of pencil-thick twigs. Next, she found a branch three times thicker and put it on the outside of the teepee firebase. "This will buy me time until I get the forearm-thick branches and larger pieces for the night," she said to the knife.

She grabbed the magnesium fire starter and used the knife to scrape the dull magnesium into the cotton ball. When the grey dust had amounted to a pile of fine powder, she used the striker side by tilting it toward the cotton and filings. She slid the knife down the striker several times until a spark caught the magnesium and then the cotton ball. The kindling burned quick, but the pencil-sized pieces were dry and caught before the kindling had gone. Before long, the teepee was alight, and Sophia was off finding firewood.

The spot she chose was next to a large rock. She decided to make camp between the rock and fire. She gathered several pine branches and stacked them to make two walls on the sides of the rock. She placed more branches over the top to make a roof and gathered pine needles to make the floor soft enough to sleep. With the fire to the front and the rock to her back, she felt safe for the night. She settled into her shelter and wrapped herself in the astronaut blanket as the woods around her absorbed the darkness of night.

Sophia was content. She may have been strayed off course by the bobcat, but she knew she could rely on her survival skills until she returned to the Hawthorn trees. She nibbled the Power Bar and kept half for the morning, allowing herself to drink half the Gatorade mixed water. She fell asleep to the sound of owls and distant yips of wild canines.

Chapter 8

SURVIVING

Sophia awoke with the fire orange glowing embers of her campfire. The pit kept the heat and fire protected. She sipped the Gatorade and nibbled at the Power Bar. She was hungry and didn't want to eat the whole bar because it was the only one. She wanted more food because she knew it would be a good day of hiking to get back to the mesa. It was her goal to make it back there before nightfall. She had to head East, and the sun was low and clear. A good indicator of the direction she needed to go. Before taking down her shelter and extinguishing the fire with shovelfuls of dirt, she took six sticks, each about six inches long, and carved notches in the end.

She headed down the mountain, the 12-gauge on her shoulder, a can of spray paint for tree marking, and her sticks. She found four flat rocks, each weighing between 5 and 10 pounds. "Perfect, Jack," she said to the knife in her pocket. She set two deadfalls and returned to her camp following the painted trees she had marked. Winston never left her side, he was trained well. Even though he was hungry he stayed next to Sophia. He had a job to do. He was her protector.

The last time she and Jonathan had gone camping as a necessity, they were by a stream. She drank the water after it was heated through and safe. Now, she was faced with trying to find a water source so that she could rehydrate, filter the water and use the rest of her Gatorade powder. She knew the stream came from the top of the mountain, so she continued to spray the trees as she went and searched for water.

Sophia happened upon a small ditch with a steady flow of water that fed a downhill stream. She wondered if that was her stream while she put the water in her LifeStraw water bottle. With the new water supply, she finished off the Gatorade water she left from the day before. She saw a cricket and snatched it to save for breakfast back at camp. Even this tiny bit of food would calm her rumbling belly. *Darn, I'm hungry,* she thought. She searched the ground for a few more but only came up with a few stinging nettles and fern shoots. She tapped a pine tree for its sweet sap and picked up a handful of pine nuts. *It's enough for breakfast,* she thought. Winston did the same, He chewed on a stick he had found, and ate some leaves off the ferns.

She headed back to camp with her bounty and rekindled the fire with a scraping of the magnesium and several handfuls of kindling. Once she had it going, she put the cricket on a stick to roast and used a rock to moisten the plants with water and cook them to rid them of any harmful bacteria or parasites. She made a sweet tasting nut mash from the sap and pine nuts and cooked it like a pancake. Once warmed, she and Winston shared her sandwich made from the cricket, the leaves and the pine-nut pancake.

Satisfied that she would find her way on the descent, she dismantled the shelter and buried the fire. She urinated on the dirt to ensure it was wet and added even more dirt. When she was confident the fire would not rekindle, she loaded her gear bag on her back, folded the blanket into a neat square, and put it in a side pocket. She headed toward the traps, following the painted trees.

***

The first deadfall was still intact. She was disappointed but disassembled it and took the sticks with her. She headed further along the descent toward the second. Being set up only a few hours prior, she didn't expect anything from either. But her empty stomach hoped for one to be a success. She skipped down the hill toward the base of a tree where she had placed the second trap. There were pine cones scattered around. Pine cones had seeds. Small critters ate seeds. Sure enough, Sophia saw the top stone flat on the base.

"Jack," she whispered. "I think I got something."

She sneaked closer to the trap. A furred tail lay lifeless outside the rock.

"A chipmunk!" she yelled. Sophia grabbed the top rock and removed the critter. "You should not have left your nest today, Chip. But thank you for your sacrifice and assisting me on my journey." She bowed her head in thanks and placed it in the garlic filled bag to get the fleas out of the fur. Sophia decided to skin it when she reached the mesa. She carried her dinner by the tail as she made her way, following the trees.

She periodically sipped the water in the LifeStraw and tapped the Gatorade powder left on her tongue. It reminded her of the paper straws with powdered candy. It was satisfying in an odd way.

When she made it to the mesa, the sun was low. Sophia used the pocketknife to field dress and skin the small chipmunk. She didn't want to chance a nighttime encounter with the bobcat, so she found a fallen tree to use as an anchor for her shelter. She gathered downed trees and stacked them. In one day, she was tired because she didn't expect to have a multi-day excursion, and thought, *In the future, I need to pack more Gatorade powder and Power Bars.* Then she laughed at herself. *Though roasted chipmunk might become a delicacy, I could get used to it.*

Sophia finished the shelter and used the bits of twigs and branches to create a log cabin-style fire since she decided to make a rock ring instead of a pit. She placed the cotton ball with magnesium powder in a nest of kindling and then stacked pencil-sized twigs in a log cabin pattern around the nest. She struck the striker and watched the fire glow. "I need to get this little guy roasting, Jack."

She took a thin stick and wet it with a bit of water and sprinkled salt and pepper on the meat. She put it through the center of the chipmunk and laid it across the top of the fire. With the shotgun on her shoulder, she went to the Hawthorn trees looking for a few fruits to add to her meal. She found three good fruits and brought them back.

She and Winston settled in her shelter as she placed her astronaut blanket on the floor to keep the warmth surrounding them. Since she had already used it, she had to be careful not to put a tear in it. She sipped her water and nibbled one of the fruits while the flames rose to encompass her dinner's body. Winston seemed to like the heat and fruit or maybe he was just being polite. He had his duty to protect Sophia and never leave her side. She was thankful for his training now. He had a purpose. She sure wished she could find her purpose in life now. Good thing she had a role model in Winston. Animals are simple creatures that know how to survive. She decided at that moment that she, Sophia Stevens, was going to be more like the wild animals, survive off the land and lead a simple life. She could do it, Hey she was already doing it now!

Placing another log on the fire, she turned the homemade skewer. The meat was charred, and the insides heated through. She wanted to make sure the other side was crisp as well. Parasites and critters went hand in hand. She nibbled on another Hawthorn fruit while watching the flames. They were warm and her hands chilled. She went to the Gear bag and put on the gloves, scarf, and hat. It was autumn and the mountain nights were cold.

When she came back to the fire, the chipmunk was ready for eating. She took the stick from the burning cabin and pulled a hind leg from the skewer. She tasted the fresh meat. She gave half the meat to Winston, and ate her share. He was happy, and he knew that he was protecting her. He knew he had to sacrifice to share food with her too. He understood survival. Winston's body kept her warm throughout the night as the fire grew dim. "Wow, this is good, Jack." As she spoke fondly to the orange knife, she cleaned the little bones and then the whole carcass The bones were crisp enough to eat as well and she and Winston ate them as potato chips before finishing the meal with the last Hawthorn fruit. Content that she had made it two days in the woods, she was ready to head home in the morning. But not before she found the X.

***

"You have to take three big steps; that's three paces from the last Hawthorn, Sophe. That's where you'll find mother nature's surprise."

"Just one surprise?" Sophia teased.

John took her hand and led her to a tree trunk that had grown over rock. The sides of the rock protruded from both sides and left a small cavern in the bottom.

***

Sophia awoke with a start. "I know where you hid it, John!" She blinked her eyes, surprised to see the sun had risen. "How long did I sleep?" She shook her head and checked her watch. "Oh, it's 7:45 in the morning."

She gathered the supplies she had used and put them back in the Gear bag. She dismantled the shelter and extinguished the fire as she had before. Since she was at the Hawthorn grove, she nibbled on the fruit as she searched for the trunk where John had taken her only last year.

"Jack, it's there!" She jogged to the trunk and let the Gear bag and gun fall to the ground beside her.

There was no X, but she decided to reach in the hole at the base. "I got something." She pulled out a plastic water bottle sealed in it was an envelope.

Sophia,

I hope you got to use your skills on this small adventure, and you spent at least one night with your Gear bag. Maybe you even got to make and use a trap for small game. If you did not, you must before going on to the next step of the hunt. But I have a suspicion you did.

Don't forget to restock it. Make a list, go to town, and get the supplies. The next step is to find an energy source for the cabin. Go back to where you came in and you will understand. You are almost

done., X marks the spot. Remember what I taught
you. Choose well.
I love you,
John

***

Darn it, This was not the treasure that she had been hoping for. This was not the end of the hunt, but it was part of the journey. Sophia was not done, she was in the middle of the test...even in death, Jonathan was training her, teaching her how to live without him. She knew she was not done with her training; she knew there was more to the test. She was tired, but thankful. Her self-discovery journey was working. Sophia was surviving.

Sophia thought about the energy source. The whole idea of going off-grid was to disconnect. She knew some people used generators, and others had systems hooked up to specialized power generation systems. She and Jonathan had a Yeti for their RV; it was solar. That was the most environmentally friendly and simple.

She decided to head back into town after she got to the cabin. There had to be an RV shop or outdoor supply store. She also needed to get a portable fridge. That would let her check another requirement off the list. "Look at me,

Jack," she said, patting the knife. Her eyes gleamed. It might have been small, but she was proving her life with Jonathan would continue. She even had to create a water system, to which she would worry about the filters when she went for the solar generator.

Sophia hiked with the shotgun poised and a smile on her face. The cabin emerged below her. The lake twinkled in the mid-morning light. There was no feeling as satisfying as surviving with her honed skills, knowing that her husband was proud. Even before she ever started.

***

She went into the cabin and put Jack in her pocket. "We need to figure out where to put the water purification unit," she said to the knife. The size seemed to be large enough that it would clean a good amount of lake water. Granted, she could boil it; the system guaranteed her health would stay uncompromised. She took the vinegar and wiped the kitchen counter again. There was room by the sink. The system would fit there, and, in the winter, she could melt snow if the need arose, and it probably would.

She knew there were several types of off-grid water purification methods.

She decided that the 13 gallon Life straw option was it. She would also use boiling, hot rocks and chlorine bleach as well. Done!

***

The idea of being alone in the woods for months excited her. The tranquility of the day was a blessing after being inundated with lawyers, doctors, and claims adjusters. She could imagine sitting in the rocker, sipping tea, and reading or crocheting. Making porridge and nibbling on the occasional chocolate drifted in and out of her consciousness. She sat on the edge of the bed, drowsy from tea and the lull that followed an adrenaline rush. It was evident that she was coming back to reality and down from the adrenaline-driven high that driving out to Idaho and the little cabin created. The anticipation was over. It was now a reality. She was there. And all she had was time and plenty of projects she wanted to do. But first, she had to go shopping.

***

Sophia had driven the Jeep CJ5 back through the rough terrain and through the stream that trickled over the rounded rocks. She noticed the roadway with towering trees and thought it would be a good idea to eventually clear some. It wasn't an issue yet, but winter was coming, and she bet there would be a fair amount of snow to keep her from making the trek from her would-be homestead to town.

The road to the town was a welcome sight. It was only her fifth day in her new life, and common luxuries were already a stress relief. But that feeling of tranquility could not be replaced. She sighed, remembering the curious squirrel and calm lake surface. It felt like home.

***

She pulled into the gas station and filled the Jeep CJ5. "I need to get an extra can of gas, just in case," she mumbled to herself. She took a red 5-gallon gas can and filled it, put it in the back of the Jeep and went in to pay for the gas. She picked up a few more Power Bars and beef jerky.

Tractor Supply was next door, so she made that her next stop. There were water jugs and fencing, as well as vegetable seeds and work gloves. She put them all into the cart. "Oh, thermal work boots!" her voice was louder than she expected and caught the attention of the cashier.

"Need help, Miss?" the older woman asked.

"I'm starting my way to the off-grid lifestyle and just found these great boots," Sophia said, shying away. "I didn't mean to be so loud."

The woman laughed. "You're the first to get excited over work boots. Usually, we get the hollers from people passing the chicks."

"Chicks?" Sophia asked.

"Yeah, we get chicks and keep them down by the farm supplies. Only one left, and we just got them yesterday."

A chick? Sophia thought. "Can I buy it?" she said.

"Sure, let me get someone to help you."

The cashier led the way back to the little chick, peeping under the heat lamp. "You'll have to keep her warm for a while. You have a fireplace or coal stove?"

"Fireplace. I have a wood stove too."

"You need to get yourself a good log splitter. And some of the creosote logs. You have a holding tank for the water?"

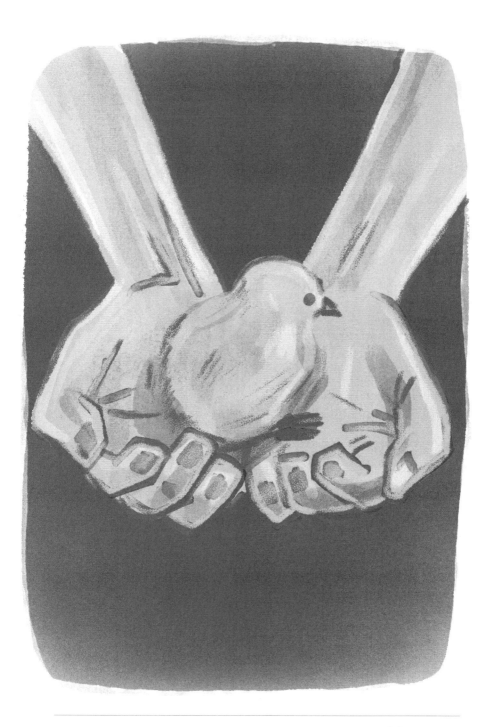

"I don't." Sophia made a list for Winter Needs on her phone.

1. Creosote logs to be burned every week
2. Holding tank for water
3. Compost bin
4. Extra dog kibble
5. Sugar
6. Chicken feed
7. Fire extinguisher
8. Snowshoes

The cashier called another employee over. He put the chick in a box, grabbed shavings, chicken feed, a heating lamp and bulb, and all the supplies they could imagine she would need to keep the chick going. She would prepare the fireplace to keep the cabin cozy in the subzero temperatures destined to grace the Idaho mountains in the coming months.

As Sophia carried the chick's box, the young man who helped her pile the supplies also helped her out to the Jeep CJ5. "You want me to load your stuff?" he asked.

"No, thank you. I'm grateful the two of you knew what I needed. It's a little overwhelming."

"Well, you come back if you have any questions. I'd be happy to help any way I can." The young man left her to put her new treasures in the back of the jeep.

The chick peeped. "Don't be nervous," Sophia cooed. "Awe, you are so sweet." A pang of guilt wafted through her. "I'm not going to eat you. We're family now." It was a declaration she felt deep in her heart. No matter what the food situation turned into, she was not going to harm that chick, even though she knew that off the grid meant that chickens were a food source. Maybe she would lay eggs.

***

Another few parking lots away, and she spotted an RV store. She pulled in, hoping they had a Yeti or a similar solar generator and filters for the water system. She left the chick on the front seat with the thermostat set at 75 degrees Fahrenheit. She forgot to ask how warm to keep it, but she couldn't control the temperature in the cabin, so it was going to be a judgment call.

An older man stood in the doorway watching Sophia fuss with the chick's cardboard box and a towel she kept in the cargo compartment. She didn't want to have it fall over from hopping in the box.

"Watch ya got there?" he called.

She swiped the back of her wrist over her forehead. Her hair was stuck to her skin from the loading of supplies to fussing with the chick. "An Orpington chick. She's unsettled."

"Well, bring her in with you. No sense letting her knockabout." He smiled. "Name's Larry."

She grabbed the handle of the box and brought the chick with her. "Well, Larry, nice to meet you. I'm Sophia. Sophia Stevens."

"Wait, you're not Jonathan's wife, are you? I heard what happened. My condolences."

Sophia wasn't sure how to respond. "I'm beginning to think my Jonathan is looking out for me more than I thought."

"He sure is. Stay here. He left something for you. I'll be right back." The old man disappeared into a back room and came back with an envelope tied to a field dressing guide. He handed it to Sophia.

"Thank you, Larry," she said. Then stuck the letter and guide into her pocket next to Jack.

"Of course. Hey, you got a dog crate or pet carrier? It would serve you well. A big enough one will keep her through winter. I assume you plan to take eggs from her next year."

"Not yet, but I was hoping to."

"I got a few. You can choose one. Won't charge you. They get left behind in the rentals and used campers." He pointed to a spot outside in a penned area filled with RVs of all sizes. "So, what can I do for you?"

"I'm looking for a solar generator. You have one?" Solar was one energy source Jonathan had impressed on Sophia. She remembered when they were camping and had to bring in the generator after a day of motorcycling.

***

"You have to look at what you're going to do in the long run, Sophe. Are you going to be nearby a town for fuel? Will you have a place to store excess? If not, you go for solar. It doesn't have to be a bright sunny day to get a bit of a charge."

"So, if I were to buy one, I would always ask for solar."

"It's a sure bet there will be sun. Who knows if you can get to a store to get any kind of gas or fuel? You can't dig up natural gas, propane, or diesel. But the sun is there to use."

"I do. A bit on the pricey side, but one of the best. How much you running on it?"

"If you have a portable fridge, that and my phone."

Larry laughed. "You'll be surprised at how many more things you'll acquire over the seasons. This one is perfect. Lithium battery, optimal charge is by solar." He pointed to the Goal Zero by Yeti. "I have one that was used. Bought from a homesteader that left. It's the largest one, too. The Yeti 6000+ is the system to have."

Sophia got goosebumps. Yeti was the brand she and Jonathan used. She already knew how it worked. Somehow her old life had prepared her for the new one before her. She clutched the chick's box to her chest and choked back tears. "I'm already familiar with this model, Larry. I'll take it."

Larry smiled. "Then I'll ring you up. Did you pick out a crate? That chick will be on the larger side. I'd suggest a German Shepard size crate to ensure she has nesting room. You can use hay, shavings, or leaves for her bedding. The Orpington chickens are hardy and fair well in colder climates. They're beautiful too. Bring in a large egg every other day or so."

"Thanks, I'll take the medium plastic one. Also, do you have any filters for a Big Berkley?"

"I'll get you twelve. Do you have a primer?"

"I don't know." Sophia thought about the silver system sitting in the army locker. There didn't seem to be any parts sitting around. She'd have to investigate the grounds more in the coming days. It was dry, and the leaves were easily moved. She could search before any big storms came in. "You know what, better to have it than not. Throw it in the pile."

Larry smiled. "You got it. I'll even throw in a pack of astronaut ice cream and freeze-dried stroganoff for you. You'd be surprised at how good it can taste after being cooped up for a few weeks."

"Thank you, Larry." She smiled back at him and took the chick to the Jeep CJ5.

Larry followed her out and fit everything in the back seats. He was able to fit the filters inside the dog crate. "You're all set. Safe travels, young lady."

"I'm sure I'll see you again, Larry. Bye!"

***

Sophia left and pulled over, anxious to read John's letter. She unfastened it from the field guide. She stuck the small booklet into her pocket and unrolled the scroll.

My Sophia,

You have been learning and growing and only in a few days. By now, you learned how to use the deadfall and stocked the cabin with food. But in order to survive,

You will need more meat, fresh meat. Get a chicken for eggs. They can feed themselves in the warmer months and provide for you. At some point, you will need to get a few more, but not this year. Your next task may take a while. I want you to procure a big game animal, preferably with fur—something to give you meat. Until then, you cannot seek the last clue to the buried treasure.

When you have secured your big game animal, use the field guide to dress it. It is important that you do not taint the meat. While you are learning to tan the hide and butcher, I want you to use a tendon to make a rope. Dry the hide, and it should be good. No salt needed; the fireplace will work. The last clue is that after the spring thaw, when *the lake is no longer frozen, take the boat to the third island in line with the sun. Bring a shovel. I want you to step off the boat and walk five paces to the North.*

Remember I love you,

John

Sophia rolled the letter and put it back in her pocket with the field guide before taking out the knife. "I have to bag a big game item and wait until spring. I can't wait to find the treasure, Jack." She hugged the knife before putting it back in her pocket and heading to the Country Store. But this waiting game is killing me! Sometimes I hate that Jonathon is still in control even when he's dead. Its killing me with anticipation! I know he's right though, I have to learn and the steps it takes me is going to take time to do it the right way. Jonathon was always so meticulous. He was and still is a great teacher—

***

Tom was stocking mason jars by the front registers. Sophia remembered him from a few days before. His face was a slight bit happier upon seeing her. "Hi, Tom. Remember me?" she said.

"I remember you, just not your name. Sorry, ma'am."

He rushed over to extend his hand this time. Sophia took it. "So, what do you think a lady with a dog and a chicken would need to survive the winter. I've got my veggies, probably come back for a few more cases, but..."

Tom gestured for her to follow. "Beans, beans, and more beans. Rice and spices, salt, and jars to keep the rodents out. Definitely potatoes, ramen, instant coffee singles, freeze-dried tomatoes, and fruits. You can dry your own meat for jerky. Oh, oil and some pepper to go with that salt."

"I need some vinegar too. Rodents, you know."

Tom brought out a 25-pound bag of black beans, a 20-pound bag of lentils, and a 50-pound bag of rice. A case of tuna and a case of sardines. He had several large containers of seasonings too. "I saw you pull in. You got room for all this?"

"I'll make room," Sophia assured as she grabbed a box of mason jars and lids and put them on the belt next to the vinegar. "Thank you, Tom."

Tom rang up her order, and Sophia was on the road. She and her new partner were on their way home. The excitement swelled in Sophia's chest. She was doing it. She spoke to the air, "John, I know you're watching over me. If there wasn't enough with the wonderful people at Tractor Supply, there just happened to be a generator I know how to use at the supply store? Thank you, Babe. I wish you were here. But I guess you are." She looked up at the sky and laughed, "And I got me a chicken."

Chapter 9

MAKING A HOME

Sophia managed to bring the water system in from the outside. It encouraged her to clean up the small building as best she could so that all cozy elements could be accomplished before she met a visitor the likes of which she didn't want. She gave the corners a good sweeping and continued outside to get all the loose debris from the building. It wasn't as bad, she thought. Behind the system, she found several rolls of RV-rated toilet paper still in their packaging. It meant the locker was a safe vessel for keeping the rodents out.

She decided to leave the chick in the box for the time being. The cabin was chilly, and she was too busy running back and forth to the outhouse and Jeep to watch the tiny critter. She brought the crate in and the large cube of shavings. It was a large cube and needed a place to be stored. The cabin was too small for that. There weren't even interior walls. Sophia put several armfuls of the pine shavings into the crate and took the cube to the army locker. It fit, snug but safe. She put the toilet paper on top and the bag of chicken feed.

It was already getting late, so she opted to call it a day. She put the gas can next to the outhouse and locked the dry goods and other supplies inside the Jeep CJ5. She brought the generator in with her. "Little chick," she said to the cardboard box, "I'll put this out tomorrow if it doesn't rain. And maybe we'll go fishing." She put Winston outside, removed the chick from the box, and cuddled it to her chest. A different sort of calm washed over her. "Hey, it's okay." She put the chick in the crate, shut the door, and started the woodstove, then let Winston back into the house. Winston sniffed the little chick, then sat and wagged his tail. He was so intuitive sometimes that Sophie could only marvel. He seemed to know that this little yellow fuzzy thing was now a part of his family. They were going to take care of Sophia, together.

She set up her YETI and the portable solar panels to charge up the power station. Then she set up the water system by the sink and took her bucket to the lake. On her way back, she saw the red squirrel again. At least she thought it was the same one. She hurried to the cabin accompanied by Winston and secured the door behind them. It was nearing dark, and she wanted to get supper. The day had been long, and she was tired. She poured the lake water into the system, saving enough for boiling.

There would be enough boiled water for Winston, the chick, and Sophia's oatmeal and tea.

While she waited for the water to boil, Sophia scooped the chick and held it to her chest. She studied the ebony eyes and gray down. "You're going to be a big girl, I hear."

The chick closed its eyes and settled in Sophia's palms.

"What should I call you?" she whispered. She thought about it until the water was boiling. When she placed the chick in the shavings, it shook and ran to the back of the carrier. "I'm not sure why, but you remind me of an Ethel." She took out a black tea bag and poured the boiling water over it. She then put a cup of oats and two spoons of sugar into the mess kit. She stirred in the water and let it sit on the stovetop until it thickened. The rest of the water she let cool on the counter. "Well, Ethel. I'm going to eat my dinner, and then we can take a nap together."

The chick trotted back and forth in the shavings. It peered at Winston and ran back to hide. Sophia ate her oats and a strip of beef jerky while she sipped her tea. She sat on the bed; legs folded so that she could get a better look at the little bird. While staples would get her through, she realized that the chick was the true beginning of their homestead.

Sophia finished her oatmeal and wiped the mess kit clean with a paper towel. She used a piece of fabric moistened with vinegar to disinfect the bowl. She tested the chick's water temperature and poured it into the chicken waterer. The chick watched her from the shadows in the crate. Sophia opened the crate and put the waterer inside.

The chick brushed against her hand. She gathered it into her fingers and brought it to her. "Hello, there, Ethel. You want to get warm and toasty?" Sophia pulled the rocker closer to the woodstove and sat with the chick in her lap. "You're a lucky chicken. You get to sit by the fire and rock in the chair." She caressed the little one's downy cheek with her thumb. "Tomorrow, we are going to clean the fireplace. And maybe, I'll get the fishing pole out to catch a fish. Would you like some fish? I know Winston would."

Sophia cradled the chick and rocked until she had to add another piece of wood to the stove. The chick had fallen asleep in her hands. The gray fluff settled down, and the tiny black eye slits closed as it napped. When she looked up she noticed that the chick naturally cuddled next to Winston's warm body and he didn't seem to mind. He and Ethel were becoming friends already. Sophia had to break them apart. Since she had to put the wood in, she placed

Ethel into the crate and closed the door. She washed her hands with a splash of lake water and then blotted them with vinegar. She peeked outside to see it was full dark. She lit the manual flashlight and went to bed.

***

Two weeks had gone by. Ethel was following Winston around like he was her surrogate mother. He loved it. She even was sounding like Winston; her peeps were in the same pattern as a barking dog.

Sophia thought on her next trip into town she would ask Larry to follow her back to the cabin and clean the chimney so she could safely use the fireplace. After losing one home to a fire, she was afraid to lose another, even more so if it was preventable. Creosote fires were a common occurrence.

She also thought that having someone know where she was in the event of an emergency was a good idea. Aunt Margie knew she was out there, so did her sister, but not the specifics. It was just foolish to overlook something so critical. Maybe she should spend time setting up the ham radio but she wanted her peace. She wanted to prove to the world she could survive on her own—off the grid.

She sat on the dock with her feet in the water. Ethel peeped in the crate beside her. Sophia held the fishing pole between her knees and watched the little orange and yellow bobber disappear beneath the water. "Looks like fish for dinner again, Ethel." Sophia reeled the now hooked fish in. "Woo, a catfish!" she hollered. Fishing off the dock brought in a fish five times out of eight. She only needed one, and she used a leftover piece of raw fish for bait. It worked great, and she was satiated.

Sophia grabbed the crate's handle, tucked the fishing pole beneath her arm, and supported the line with the fish wriggling as she headed toward the cabin. She stopped at a flat rock that she used to knock out the fresh catch so she could sever the spine. Then she split the belly and took out the insides, and placed them in a mason jar for the next day. Jonathon taught her this. He was such a kind soul, and even felt bad about killing a fly or a spider. All life, even a scorpion had purpose and should be celebrated. Sophia thanked the fish as she did with all the animals she used to survive. This was the best way to live, to be thankful and live off the grid.

The fish was as long as her arm. She cut it in half and then took a chunk of the flesh for Winston. She would feed the fast-growing chick bits of hers while she ate as they had all become dinner companions. She went back to the water to rinse her hands and the knife.

After carrying the crate inside, she went back for the fish with a cast iron frying pan she found hidden beneath the floorboards. There were also two hurricane lamps, fuel, and a bag of candles. She took to using a candle at night, but the glow from the fireplace was enough to light the cabin in a yellow-gold hue. That light warmed Sophia's heart and mind. The simple life gave her time to reflect.

✷✷✷

"I got one!" Sophia shouted. "John, look."

"That's a big one," Jonathan said, smiling at Sophia's joy. "We'll throw it on the fire. A little salt and garlic."

"Salt's bad for you," she teased.

"I'm not worried about a little salt if it makes that fish taste as good as I remember catfish tasting. Now, can you get it off the hook, or do you want me?" He teased.

"I'll do it." Sophia stepped on the fish and squatted. She took wiggled the hoot loose and maneuvered it out of the catfish's mouth without having to touch the whiskers. "See."

Jonathan chuckled. "You could have just used the end of your shirt to hold them down. But it worked, and that's what matters. Come on, let's pack up."

They were camping by the Colorado River. The night was cool after the long hot day under the blazing sun. Not a cloud drifted. They had gone back to the camper and wrapped the fish in foil. John put it at the edge of the coals.

"Look at those stars," Sophia said.

"Lake Havasu was built with no streetlights in the town. You get to enjoy all twenty-four hours here." He glanced at Sophia. "With all the stars and galaxies shining above us, you are still the brightest star, Sophe."

She glanced at him. "You're a smooth talker, Jonathan Stevens." She rolled over and kissed his cheek. "Don't burn the fish."

Jonathan got up, brought back the foil packet, and presented it to her, "Perfection."

***

Sophia flipped the fish and seasoned it with garlic powder and salt. The aroma made her stomach grumble. She hadn't eaten a regular meal since she returned to the cabin. She managed to procure red and white paints to paint the cabin with the red, the white on the trim. She got the outhouse coated in white paint and even fashioned a sheet out of a few yards of fabric. She had project after project. Sixteen days she cleaned, straightened, and worked. But for sixteen days, she neglected the basic needs of fueling her body.

Her stomach rumbled again. "Fish and oatmeal it is, Jack. And one of those Whatchamacallit bars." She got the mess kit out and put a handful of oats in it with some purified water. She added raisins instead of sugar.

She used the lid of her bin as a table and lit the hurricane lamp. The fireplace had a low fire keeping the chill October air at bay. To her surprise, the cabin was sturdy and didn't leak when it had rained for two days, and there were no big areas for drafts. The hardest part of life was keeping after Ethel. Winston knew what living free meant.

Sophia took the orange knife from the nest of blankets she used to keep it from Ethel's sight. The chick learned to come by its name inside the cabin but pecked at all things moving or not. Sophia took the knife to the makeshift table and set it on the opposite side of the lid.

"Catfish for dinner, Jack. Maybe I'll have Rooibos tea with dessert. Do you remember when I introduced you to it?" She laughed, "It smelled fined, but when you sipped it, your face crinkled, and I thought you were going to spit it out." She sighed, "but you didn't. You put like six spoons of honey and half and half in the mug. That tea always reminds me of you."

Sophia nibbled the fish and oats until they disappeared. Her thoughts drifted to how she could build a pen for Ethel outside during the day and inside at night. Her other thoughts focused on the coming winter and having enough wood to get through it. "I think for this first winter, I'm going to have chop up a fallen tree. Good thing I have a chain saw. If I get three cords of seasoned, then I can get ahead for next year. All the wood I cut now will be ready." She took a spoon of oatmeal. "I need to get my essential living projects done soon. It really feels like home, right Jack?"

The chick was nestled into her shavings, the fish gone. Sophia let the woodstove go out and added another log to the fireplace. Unless it was ridiculous cold, there was no reason to have the two elements going. She stoked the fire and cleaned up her dinner. The fish bones she saved for the curious red squirrel that hung around each morning. She discovered it digging the bones she had buried after the first fish. It solved the problem of getting rid of the carcass because she didn't want to draw in larger critters. She put it away from the cabin while the squirrel watched and then went about her projects. The squirrel scampered off, and the carcass was gone. It was the perfect situation. It was easier with Winston because he ate his raw—bones and all.

After the oatmeal and fish, she determined the entire candy bar would be too much. She cut off a bite-sized piece, brewed her Rooibos tea, and sat back in the rocker by the fire. The flames danced against the stones. Their glow performed with the shadows. She let the candy dissolve on her tongue, taking small sips of tea. The chocolate mingled with the earthy flavor delivering the simple treat she remembered from childhood.

Her grandmother gave her a square of milk chocolate and a steaming mug of red rooibos tea. "Eat and drink this together for the richness that comes from the earth's gifts."

Why did I remember that?

Sophia put the camping cup aside. She straightened up the counter area, made sure the portable fridge was closed and grabbed Jack.

Before she blew out the lamp and tucked Jack into the sleeping bag, she peered at Winston and the sleeping chick and whispered, "Good night, Ethel and Winston."

Chapter 10
THE FIRST SNOW

It was November, Sophia awoke to the fireplace out. The cabin's cooled air stung her face. Her body was warm and toasty in her sleeping bag. Winston lay at her feet. She hated to slide out of it, but she had to light both fires. It would also heat the cabin quicker. She lit the fireplace first and then threw a few split pieces into the woodstove.

"Good morning, Jack," she said to the knife as she tucked it in her pocket before opening the crate and then the outside door to let the chicken roam free to do her business and find breakfast.

"Oh, wow, Jack."

The lake sparkled, clear diamonds on navy water. The shores were covered in a blanket of fresh snow. The towering pines had snow caps with crystalline branches. The ground was blanketed with white powder. "This is breathtaking," she sighed. She wrapped an alpaca throw she'd picked up at the Country Store during her last trip and draped it over her shoulders. The awe coaxed her onto the porch.

The red squirrel made tracks from behind the Jeep CJ5 as it scampered to its usual tree. The creature stayed focused on Sophia. It had become brazen and exemplified its trust each day by staying longer and getting closer. Sophia went inside and grabbed an acorn from the pile she gathered to befriend the critter.

She tossed it to him, and he leaped for the treat. He turned it around and carried it in his mouth up the tree to a low branch. Sophia didn't want him in the cabin and only gave him one treat on the days he appeared. She wouldn't set out food or lure him closer. The squirrel climbed down the tree, flattened in the snow, and watched her. It didn't seem to care that Ethel was pecking around.

"Come back tomorrow, and you can have another," Sophia called. "If you find any walnuts let me know."

She ducked back inside to start her breakfast. She opened a can of Spam and took down the frying pan. She put a pat of butter in before placing it on the stove. While it melted, she grabbed the flour, sugar, and water. She mixed the three together and made a sort of pancake, dumped it in the pan, and laid the sliced Spam on the side.

She boiled her water in a kettle she'd picked up at Larry's RV store. He had another couple freebies for her:

a drum for gasoline with a hose for the Jeep and a water collection drum with a stainless-steel spigot. She just had to fashion a gutter to collect the water. It was going to be her project for the week, but the snow altered her plan.

The food was cooked and on her plate in time for her to shed the throw. She put another log in the fireplace and kept the woodstove burning with a few smaller pieces. The cabin was warm, and she wanted it to stay that way. Learning to regulate the temperature with logs was a new skill she had to perfect. If she was going to get through the winter without freezing. That and she worried about Ethel, her egg source.

She ate her pancake with a sprinkle of chocolate chips and sipped the coffee. It hadn't taken long to become accustomed to having instant coffee and thin pancakes. They were staples she started to crave. *A strip of bacon wouldn't be bad,* she thought. And like that, she created a new shopping list. With the temperatures dropping, she could keep foods easier. Once winter came, the woods would be her freezer. She could count on the Jeep CJ5 to keep things frozen and safe.

Thanksgiving was around the corner. She had promised her sister the holiday back when she moved into the cabin.

She grabbed Jack from the fabric nest on the bed. "And how many days until then?"

She unplugged her phone from the generator and moved it outside with the solar panels in full sun. She used the bin lid that was her table as a protective shield against the snow. Getting the generator wet was not a question she thought to ask. She went back inside to check her calendar and tidy the cabin. Tidying the cabin had become a necessity. She enjoyed the simple elegance the home touches gave to the little place.

She took Ethel's crate outside and cleaned it with a bucket of lake water. The normal thing to do was let it dry in the sun, but now it had to go in front of the fireplace. She went to the outhouse and wiped it down inside and out with the broom. Then came sweeping the outside of the cabin. When finished, she would tap the broom in the snow to clean it off before bringing it inside to dry by the fire. As was her habit, she boiled a bucket of lake water and used a washcloth with a bar of antibacterial soap to wash. She would do her hair when she was done for the day because she, too, needed to dry by the fire.

Once the daily routine was finished, she set out to find food. She took the shotgun and a handful of shells with her for safety. Her biggest desire was to catch as many fish as she could today because she had to stockpile for the winter months and she looked forward to it. She cast the fishing pole in the water and propped it on a stand she fashioned out of a branch. It was lunchtime, and still no bites. She secured her pole and headed up to the cabin.

A black shadow moved behind the outhouse.

"Ethel, come," Sophia called. "Ethel."

The chicken was under the Jeep CJ5 and had no interest in leaving. Winston was gone, and the woods were silent. The snow made it quieter still. The black shadow brushed against the overgrown bushes that grew around the sides of the white building. She had left them wild out of respect for nature. It was the overgrown branches that let her know something was there.

"Yah, get," she yelled from the dock. Whatever it was had been closer to the cabin than she thought. "Crap," she whispered. Then she remembered the shotgun on her shoulder and the shells in her pocket. She loaded her shotgun and pumped one into the chamber.. She scanned the woods for any movement. Nothing. Several clumps of snow fell from the trees as the midday sun melted the branches, but no life forms. Ethel ventured nearer to the porch.

Worried for her safety, Sophia sidled up the dock toward the bird. She kept focus on the outhouse bushes, with glances in all other directions. It didn't take long before she reached Ethel, scooped her in her arms, and slipped inside the cabin, bolting the door.

Still worried about Winston, Sophia opened the forest green curtains to keep watch. Since the window faced the outhouse, she waited, just in case. Her afternoon hunger was replaced with fear. It was her first encounter, the one John said she should use, big game for winter. Only then could she advance to the last step to claim the treasure. She took a deep cleansing breath and focused back on the bushes. She looked for a pot and lid to pound to make some noise. She was too far away.

Nothing.

She laid the loaded gun on the bed. She couldn't stay captive for the rest of the night. Ethel's shavings were in the outhouse, and Winston was somewhere. Sophia grabbed the gun. She had to complete the steps to the scavenger hunt. She crept out of the cabin door and scanned the three sides.

Nothing.

She continued toward the outhouse, creeping, inching her way to the door. Keeping watch from both sides, she went inside and locked the door. There was no window. She took the bucket she used for shavings and filled it, secured the locker, and unbolted the door. With the bucket handle hung over her arm, she raised the gun to shooting position and stepped out of the security of wooden walls into the open whiteness. She felt like a target. She crept faster toward the cabin door, keeping an eye on the outhouse and back of the cabin that led into the woods.

As Sophia stepped onto the porch, she saw the black snout with a tan ring before the head made its way onto the porch from the other side. The grizzly bear stood on its hind legs. It was huge, pointy teeth, and claws so long and sharp they looked like knives. Then Winston came out of nowhere and lunged at the bear. The bear roared and swiped his massive paw with claws extended. Winston leaped backwards, barely escaping certain death.

"Winston, come back. Please Winston," Sophie yelled, but Winston was in his moment of protecting her. He circled behind the bear and jumped on his back biting at his neck. The bear roared again and whirled around, throwing Winston about 30 feet into the yard. Winston hit with a thud, the wind knocked out of him as he lay limp.

"Oh no, Winston," cried Sophie.

Without thinking, Sophia pulled the trigger. The bear went to all fours, roaring in pain. Blood poured from a gunshot wound in the head right next to his eye. Sophia fired again. The bear stumbled and lay on its side by the Jeep. This time Sophia had hit it in straight in its face. Her heart thumped, and her breath left her, but the shavings were in the bucket, and she still had her wits about her. She put the shavings down and went to the bear, gun raised. Had she stayed inside, she would not have seen the bear. The window was on the wrong side of the cabin. She needed another. There wasn't even a peephole in the door. It was necessary to see what was around.

She counted to a hundred with another chambered shell. If the bear were alive, it would meet the gun first. She pumped one more round, ready to fire. No movement. She stepped through with caution, her back against the wall. Drops of red littered the snow. She peered around the windowless side of the cabin and then the other. Satisfied that there were no others, she grabbed the generator and put it back inside. Winston ran up behind her and paused by the bear, sniffing to make sure it couldn't hurt his Sophie. Winston had saved Sophie's life and she saved his. They were a team.

Sophia took Jack from her pocket. "I did it, Jack. Now to remember how to tan this big guy and learn to use every part." She approached the bear, still cautious, and knelt beside it with the gun slung over her shoulder. This was the real circle of life. "Thank you for providing for me," she said to the bear. She stroked its head and pulled the guide for field dressing big game from her small backpack.

When she went on the first scavenger hunt, she needed the Gear bag. But since then, she had been creating a homestead as each later hunt urged. The bear would satisfy one of Jonathan's requirements: secure red meat for the winter months, a leather hide, and claws for cutting. Sophia dressed the bear, drained the blood. She would use the organ meat to catch more fish, but first she would have to hang the meat to drain. It took her the day to skin the bear and tan the hide. Good thing she had her tent. She had to smoke the meat somewhere, since she did not have time to build a smokehouse this season. She had enough food for the winter now. She took the empty food cans and cut slabs of fat to melt down into oil. As it melted, she thought of all the great uses for bear fat; lubricating her gun and knife, preserving the leather, and using in her oil lamps for light. Sophia found some canning jars in the cabin to hold the oil.

Chapter 11

THANKSGIVING

"Tomorrow's Thanksgiving, Jack," Sophia sighed. She had her monthly check-in call with her sister two days prior, and their plans were canceled. A snowstorm was expected. It had started when Sophia went to bed and was supposed to linger long into Thanksgiving Day.

Sophia was stuck at the cabin. She shot a wild turkey and dressed it. Sophia was living off the land now and using the plants around the forest as her garden. Good thing she had found some wild squash a few weeks ago. She used cinnamon and spices to make it taste like a real pumpkin pie. She substituted bear oil for butter.... She made mashed potatoes and gravy. She baked a loaf of bread, sliced, and toasted it to crumble for her dressing. She even used the edible plants she picked in the forest to herb the turkey and her dressing. It was turning out to be a real Thanksgiving meal after all.

It was her first Thanksgiving without her family or Jonathan. The bear attack was the only one of its kind, but Sophia lost the security she felt when she first arrived. Looking over her shoulder had become natural.

Winston waited at the door. They had developed a routine. Sophia got up and scoped the property before letting him out to roam. She would use the time to place the generator, toss an acorn to Mitch, the name she gave to the squirrel. Then she would hurry to the outhouse to use the facility, and gather any needed supplies before heading back to the cabin. Since the snow was mounting fast, she scattered Ethel's shavings in her compost bin and dumped the new inside. She shoveled a path through the snow to pull supplies and a case of water from the Jeep CJ5 which was now her refrigerator and pulled Jack from her pocket, eager to hold him by the fire with a hot cup of black tea sweetened with a spoon of honey. She had made rice a few days before and had a small bit left. It promised to make a nice mid-morning meal with a bit of stewed bear. She put it in her mess kit to warm.

She tucked Jack in the fabric nest on the bed. When she made her bed, she relocated him to the foot of the bed by the rocker. The soft glow from the fire and warm wood made the tension in her shoulders ease. She ate and sipped, watching the snow fall outside the kitchen window.

"Babe, we're going to be late," Sophia called. She was sitting in her Jeep CJ5. The back was filled with suitcases and presents.

Jonathan rushed to climb into the passenger side. "We're staying at your sisters for dinner and then,"

"Then we give hugs and kisses as we head to the airport for our 8:30 flight."

"And when do we depart Galveston?"

"With no delays? 10 am."

"This is going to be a blast. Taking a cruise through the Panama Canal and seven ports of call." He grabbed her hand and kissed her wrist.

"Fourteen days isn't long enough. One lifetime isn't enough. You're my everything. You know that don't you?"

He smiled; his eyes glistened. "I know, but we have this one amazing life. And together, we will make it last an eternity."

They drove to her sisters in Southeastern Idaho. It was uncanny weather, a Thanksgiving in the seventies. Sophia preferred it because she had a flight to catch, but it still disturbed her. She worried about climate change.

Global warming tugged at her heart. Jonathan saw wildlife displaced by wildfires and floods. He took part in rehoming birds and others that required human care.

***

"You had a heart of gold, John," she whispered to the fire.

Winston had fallen asleep at her feet, so she was careful not to disturb him. The honey had blended through the tepid water. When she was a kid, her mother gave her almond cookies that she liked to dunk in her cooled tea. She would always nibble the almond off before dipping the actual cookie. As an adult, she still liked them but broke them in half to make the dunking easier and the bites smaller.

The snow continued into the evening and through the night. Sophia grabbed a handful of nuts and another of chocolate chips and munched them while she sliced a piece of bear meat and scooped up some leftover squash from lunch the day before. She place everything in her mess kit and warmed them over the flames in her fireplace. She lit a hurricane lamp with bear oil and decided to fiddle with the emergency weather radio.

***

During the holidays Sophia had put a tin star that she made from her canned food cans on top of the Douglas fir tree outside her door. She had gone out to the outhouse on Christmas morning and when she returned, she found her Christmas present. Ethyl laid her first egg, and Ethyl was now laying one egg a day. Sophia, had to slyly remove it from her box daily so that Ethyl would lay another. This was a treat for her, and a surprise when it first happened. Eighteen weeks went by so fast living off the grid, happily living life in nature, and she realized she was happy.

The snow deepened over the next couple of months. She knew that it sometimes snowed until May in Idaho, but she had enough canned foods, dry goods, dog kibble, and chicken feed to last the winter. She had stockpiled cases that she kept in the Army locker and Jeep CJ5. She figured there would be about 120 days they would be snowed in. She and Winston and Ethyl would be fine.

"Add another thirty, Jack. That's what you told me the homesteaders had to do. In Alaska, they had to plan six months in some places. I have 150 cans of vegetables and an equal number of canned meats, jerky, and then oats, flour, sugar, cornmeal, and the bear. I should be okay."

John had told her that homesteading in winter needed math. You had to look at the weather trends and add a month's worth of supplies in order to get through. You needed: canned protein, canned vegetables, dried goods like rice and raisins, extra water filters, extra batteries, more chopped wood, dried milk powder, first aid supplies, fat like lard or oil, animal foods, and Tylenol, a thermometer, and cough drops.

The last trip back over the stream proved difficult. The water was higher, and ice had thickened on both sides. Sophie took her axe and chopped ice free and hauled it back to the front of the cabin where she constructed a small igloo, the perfect freezer. She hung tin cans over the front so that if any animal disturbed it, she would hear and chase them away.

With the recent storms, the snow had mounted over the pass. The tires spun, and she worried she would get in a situation she wasn't experienced enough to get out of. Jonathan was the one with the off-roading skills. And even then, she wasn't confident he would venture through the mountain snows unless it were dire.

She knew the off-road skills: use low lock, always have a floor mat and shovel to put under a spinning tire to get out of a situation, have your Gear backpack in the vehicle with you. Have a portable floor jack tire wrench, winch on the vehicle, and know how to cook on the engine. She could gather snow in her water bottle and boil it on a hot engine. John had shown her how. She also had the solar battery trickle charger to hook up to the Jeep's battery to keep it working.

"Think this new year is going to bring good times, Jack." Sophia put the knife in the rocking chair. "I'm mixing some of the leftover bear fat with the cornmeal and water and sugar. Want some?" She made the batter into pancakes until there wasn't any left. She had seven small cakes. She took two and handed one to Winston, who was at her feet.

First, she started the woodstove; then, the pan came off the wall. Food was cooked, and then Sophia sat in the rocker and tossed a portion of something into Ethel's crate. Sophia cherished Ethel.

Sophia was interrupted by a thump on the roof. The snow came steady, and the wind picked up. She grabbed the manual flashlight and wound it until the light shined as bright as any other. She pulled on her boots and parka before heading outside to see what it was.

She unbolted the door, but a gust of wind thrust it inward, knocking Sophia back. She tried to steady herself and push it closed. As the heat was sucked out of the small space, she fought even harder to close the door. "I bet it's a tree, Jack," she said.

The chick huddled in its crate. Winston stayed at her side. Sophia bolted the door and wrapped the sleeping bag around her body. She sat on the floor with her back to the wall space across from the window.

"I woke up once in fear. It won't happen again," she said. She put Jack into her parka pocket and called Winston to her. "Winston, come."

The dog came to his name.

Sophia scooped him up and clutched him to her chest for warmth, Jack still in her pocket. She drifted to sleep, listening for the wind to tear the little cabin apart.

***

"What do you need for a seven-day snow-in?" John grilled.

Sophia smiled. They were in the mile-high city of Denver, and the snow was falling for hours. "I need food that won't spoil like canned meats, fruits, and vegetables. At least one can per meal per person. Sugar, water, Gatorade powder, dry cereals, granola bars, and jerky. Batteries and a flashlight, a hand crank radio or HAM radio, water filters, or iodine tablets. Oh, and a fire starter."

"I'm proud of you, Sophia. It's not easy to remember."

Chapter 12

ETHEL

It was March 21st. Spring was official, and the thaw had started. Sophia ventured out in the Jeep CJ5 with bags of cleaned cans, ready to recycle, and a phone list of supplies she needed. Among them was plywood for the roof where a broken branch landed on the roof. She climbed on top to check the damages weeks prior. Now that she was headed to civilization, she was going to see if Larry had any suggestions.

She stopped at the RV store first. Larry was spreading salt when she pulled in.

"Hey, Larry."

"Sophia. I was wondering if you'd make it out yet."

"It's spring. The sun decided to let me have a day."

He laughed, "What can I get you?"

"Advice more than anything tangible."

"I'm all ears."

Sophia explained the roof and cedar row. "The tree won, and I need a long-term repair."

"I'll come by this week. It's supposed to be warm. I'll bring corrugated metal roofing. We'll put plywood over the damage and the roofing over the whole thing. That should keep you for a good 20 years."

"Thanks, Larry."

"You still have that chick?"

"Ethel? She's a full-grown chicken now. She's my girl."

"I look forward to meeting her."

"See you," Sophia called to him as she hopped in the Jeep CJ5.

It felt good to see a friend. It had been a long winter. She was sure it was longer than it needed to be because she wasn't confident driving on unpaved roads and over icy waterways. She headed to the Country Store for her supplies and to check in with her sister.

***

After she got off the phone with her sister, Sophia took a cart inside. There were ice fishing supplies with drill augers. She decided to grab one because the lake wouldn't thaw for weeks and was certain the bears were still in hibernation. There hadn't been any footprints—only hoof marks from the deer and Mitch's tracks.

She smelled fresh bread and headed to the bakery. They had racks of cooling Italian loaves. "Excuse me, can I have one of those, please?" she called back to the young man bagging them. He handed her one. "Thank you." She sniffed the bread through the air holes, her mouth watered. There were urns with hot chili and soups. Sophia filled a large container of each.

As she filled her cart with canned meats and vegetables, she added stews, soups, and Spaghetti-O's. A case of macaroni and cheese and a pack of Oreos completed her quest.

"Powdered milk can go a long way," a familiar voice offered.

"Tom?" She turned around, pleased to see him. He'd filled out over the winter. His jaw was squared, and his beard had thickened.

He was stocking boxes of dry milk and handed her one.

"Thanks, how've you been?"

"Working, shoveling. I'll meet you at the register."

Sophia had Tom put the hot stuff in a separate bag with the warm bread on top. He followed her to the Jeep CJ5 and loaded her stuff in the back. "Sorry, I have to get rid of these cans," she said, pointing to the bags in the back seat. "They're clean."

"We have recycling bins around back. You can sort your stuff in there, just no bags."

"Thanks again. See you in another few weeks."

"Yup." He waved and went back inside the store.

Sophia drove to the back. She dumped her cans in the appropriate bin and headed home. *It's great that they recycle here,* she thought. She was glad she had procured the compost bin last autumn.

* * *

When Sophia pulled next to the cabin, she took her store items inside and made dinner after lighting the woodstove. She put the chili in her mess kit and the soup in the fridge; the bread she put on the counter and covered it with the skillet. It was a last-minute realization that had her take the precaution. "Ethel, you be good and stay off the counter." Every day since December 25th, Ethel was laying an egg. She had her routine, wake up and lay an egg in her box, then go about her merry day playing with Winston.

After she sorted the groceries, she planned to use for the week, she brought the generator in and settled into her sweatsuit. They were worn from repeated use as pajamas, but they were warm and comfortable. She gave them a good washing in boiling water with vinegar and her antibacterial soap every week, even in the winter. She hung the suit by the fire or the clothesline she fashioned from the Home Depot twine stored away from when she first arrived. It was tied between two trees next to the dock.

Today was the first she would wear the washed pajamas for the week. They were crisp but smelled like soap. It was a good smell. She took the skillet off the stove and changed it out with the mess kit. She ripped a quarter of the loaf and put it in the pan to warm. She took a smaller piece and handed it to Ethel.

"This is good."

The bird took her dinner and pecked it apart at Sophia's feet. Sophia laughed and carried her dinner to the rocking chair. As she ate, she rocked. It was involuntary but a sign of internal joy. She planned to make a bigger stock of food for the following year. She planned to add more dinners. Foods that made her smile, not just to fill her belly. She survived, but her purpose was to live.

Sophia remembered John's letter. She had memorized it over the winter. The lake was thawed enough for her to take the fiberglass boat to the third island. She grabbed the shotgun, a pocket full of shells, Jack, and secured Winston and Ethel in the cabin.

With the gun on her shoulder, she headed to the boat, flipped it over, and stepped in. She hadn't been in it for months. Sophia pushed off with the oars and rowed her way through the thawing water. She had her Gear bag and life vest, so she felt confident in the journey.

***

When she reached the third island, Sophia hopped ashore and pulled the boat onto the land. She tied the rope to a tree that was no more than a foot inland. She faced north and did her paces. Before her was a cave with a pine needle path, she lit her manual flashlight and headlamp before she stepped into the blackness of the cave. About twenty feet in, she spotted a shovel. And then, before her eyes were two large, charred branches making an 'X.' Sophia's heart pounded in her throat. "John, I found it," she yelled. Her voice reverberated off the cave walls. She pushed the branches aside and dug into the non-compact dirt.

The shovel struck metal.

She stooped down to dig with her hands. She found a latch to a metal footlocker. As she opened it, her eyes welled up with tears. Gasping for air, she was so excited, her emotions overtook her. Inside was a library of separated Ziploc bags full of all types of seeds for food planting, a journal of Jonathan's lists which, at a glance, checked out with hers, a picture of them harvesting from their first garden, even a deed to the property. And on the side was a note.

Sophia,

You get an "A" for learning from my years of educational talks. You survived, and now you will thrive. Grow these seeds and the homestead we always dreamed of having is now, officially yours. Live your best life, and remember I love you.

Always yours,

Jonathan

Sophia left the cave sobbing with happiness as she carried the footlocker filled with treasure. Jonathan lived on through his teachings. His love was encapsulated in that small cave in the middle of their lake. She rowed back to shore with a warm heart and a plan to start growing for the coming season.

Chapter 13
ANOTHER YEAR

ANOTHER YEAR

The weather was not as kind over the next year. There were high winds, torrential rains, and summer drought. Larry had fixed the roof, which Sophia was thankful for because had he not, the limbs and debris that landed on the cabin would have destroyed the shale tiles. Her first season of crops yielded enough for her to eat, feed Ethel and Winston, and dry for the winter months. But she had enough seeds to last years.

She learned to use the boat to get more fish and sit in it after drilling a hole in the ice with the auger. She even managed to catch a few fish. Despite the harsh weather, Sophia was thankful. She had friends eager to help her learn. Hunting deer, turkey, pheasants, moose and using all their body parts to so that she could survive. She never forgot to thank the animals as she used them for her survival.

A people that understood the value of nature surrounded her. Each day she looked out on the lake in wonder. There was no pollution. From what she saw, it was untouched, except by her. Of course, there was runoff. But for the most part, she got to live in harmony with the land, air, and water. She didn't take more than she needed, nor did she mindlessly discard her waste.

Recycling and composting were a big part of her life. She raised Ethel to be a free-range bird. The feed was for those long winter months where the snow was deeper than her girl. Even the squirrel learned that one acorn a day was enough. He had to do his part and scavenge because his stockpiles resulted in planted trees, flowers, and shrubs. She was a part of the cycle of life.

Winston loved the wilderness as well. He learned to play with the birds, the butterflies, and of course, Ethyl.

Sophia even called her sister on a regular schedule. It was another new year, and she was still learning, exploring. Her decision to go off-grid started with Jonathan but was now a part of who she was. She enjoyed small hikes around the cabin and along the lake's shore. The tinkling rain on the metal roofing sent her to sleep on rainy nights. It was all part of who she had become.

Chapter 14
THE IDES OF MARCH

Sophia grabbed the machete and shotgun. She had three shells left. It was a means of protection rather than food gathering. After following Mitch, she learned where to find buried nuts. She relied on the stockpile she'd gathered over the months rather than hunting. "Has it been months?" she asked herself and called back over her shoulder, "Be back with dinner, Jack."

She spotted Mitch in his usual spot. Sophia pulled an acorn from her pocket and held out her hand. Mitch scampered toward her. She bent down so her hand was ground level. The red squirrel stepped up and accepted her offering. He took it to a rock beside the dock and dined while he watched Sophia make her way to the thick woods behind the cabin. She knew Mitch would not follow her because he did not venture into the thick woods, He knew better. He was somewhat domesticated He would play with Winston and Ethyl in front of their Cabin.

Sophia had traps setup about a mile away from the cabin, It was in an area where Mitch did not venture. Somehow he knew and so did Ethyl and Winston, not to go there. One trap was a flat rock and stick called a deadfall, another was a form of snare that she fashioned after learning from too many failed attempts. It worked once on a mouse. She also had a net in the water. It was a good bet there would be a fish or two. She hadn't checked on it in a few days. After the first week of no jerky and sardines she wanted more than vegetables. She was hungry. She checked the nets several times a day only to get discouraged. Now she let three days go by before going to the area at the end of the dock where she fastened the first point. It was easy to break the ice from there.

***

The lake's spoils had been good over the summer. It was her second winter; Sophia knew there were fish. It took skill and time to learn how to get them. The biggest skill of them all is patience, she thought. She figured the net would come last. The fish didn't bite during the midday and hung out in the warming water. Every so often, she threw a handful of Ethel's feed into the area where the net was anchored. She was surprised the first time it worked.

The warm waters and boat trips to find new schools relaxed her. She even caught a few crayfish and mussels.

She reminisced about the sun and warmth as she ventured into the knee-deep snowy woods behind the cabin. It was March, again. And the last call with her sister ended with her sister's warning, "There's a blizzard coming." Sophia knew the late-season storms dumped over a foot of snow. This would be the third, and the month wasn't over.

***

The snow kept coming late into April. There were feet of snow blocking the roads, keeping Sophia from driving into town. She would miss another call to her sister. The temperatures warmed enough during the day for the melt to cause the streams to overflow their banks.

Sophia avoided the area behind her cabin because the snow-melt caused the mud to act like quicksand. She got stuck up to her ankle once. She didn't want a repeat or worse. What if it went to her knees or hips? She stayed around the lake and checked the net. But to Sophia's surprise, she let Ethel out for her morning romp and discovered an egg. Ethel had been feeding Sophia for two weeks. Even though it was only 3 or 4 eggs a week, it was more than Sophia had before. She was grateful.

***

Sophia ventured out toward the egress on foot. She took the shotgun with her. It was May, and still, she hadn't bothered driving out. By the time she finished her daily chores and settled down with her tea, she didn't mind staying home. It was cozy. She even started drying plants by the fire. They made great craft projects. She'd made a porch chair from fallen branches and twigs that she soaked in the lake to soften. And she had Jack, Winston, and Ethel.

She tried her hand at making a grass rug but wasn't pleased with the outcome. Still, she used it in the outhouse. "No waste," she told Ethel. When she had fish, she shared. If Ethel didn't finish hers, it was saved for Mitch.

***

Finally, Sophia knew she should try and drive out of the mountains. When she reached the stream, the roadway disappeared under a strongly flowing barrier of water making passage impossible. Sophia's heart sank. "What am I going to do?" She sat at the water's edge and cried. Winston licked her cheek.

***

"Have you seen this woman?" Sophia's sister asked the clerk at the Country Store. She and Margie stared at the young man with eyes like glass, the kind of stare that begs for hope.

Tom was quick to answer, "Yeah, she's the lady from the wildfires. I see her every few months." His voice faltered, "Why? Did something happen?"

"She checks in," Sophia's sister lamented. "She always calls me. At least monthly. I haven't heard from her in over five months."

"When was the last time you saw her?" Margie urged.

"Come to think of it; it's been a while, like spring break. She took whole cases of cans. I was the only one here to unload the truck and stock. There were cases of vegetables. She took like ten of them. Didn't even care what was in them."

"Did she say anything?" Sophia's sister asked, her voice higher in pitch.

"No, she just offered to help me out. I put them in her jeep."

"She isn't much of a talker. She just kind of gets stuff, smiles, and is polite."

★★★

Larry's truck roared over the long grass field. The tires spun in the still drying earth. The recent downpours kept the ground spongy. He honked his horn repeatedly. Two camouflaged ATVs rumbled behind him. A police light flashed from one with a siren sounding.

Winston barked, running toward the truck. Sophia stood on her porch. She hadn't seen Larry in months. Aunt Margie and Sophia's sister Connie waved from Larry's cab. He slowed the truck, and Connie threw the door open and leaped out. She stumbled toward Sophia.

"Oh, my God, you're safe." She ran her arms out.

"Connie? What's going on?" Sophia asked, dumbfounded.

"It's been half a year. You've no idea how long it's taken to get to you," Connie blurted. "I was so worried..." she reached Sophia and pulled the thin woman into her arms. "Sophia, I love you so much."

"I love you, too." Sophia was still confounded. "The egress washed out, and I couldn't get back to town. I don't have service for my cell until then."

Connie grabbed her face; her eyes focused on her sister's. "You don't have to explain, honey. We know. If it hadn't been for Larry being at the right place in the right moment, we'd still be looking for a detour to get to the cabin."

"I'm sorry, I didn't mean to worry you," Sophia said.

The ranger broke in, "No need to apologize. You've made quite the homestead here. It looks like you've faired quite well."

Ethel ran out of the cabin and into the field, and Larry got out of his truck. "Is that the chick?"

Sophia nodded. "Larry? How are you?"

He shrugged. "Good now that your sisters got you. That little lady's been all over asking about you."

"Thank you." Sophia went to the older woman climbing from the truck. "Aunt Margie, what's going on?"

The ranger offered Sophia a granola bar. She took it. "Last April, the thaw brought flooding along with higher-than-average rainfall. That washed out a lot of homesteaders, as you would guess. The exit from your cabin was one of the hundreds that needed repair to get vehicles in and out. Until Tom at the Country Store and Larry confirmed they had visual or personal contact with you, we had no proof of your whereabouts. Confirmed persons take precedence. We know they were there prior, and it is our duty to locate and rescue."

Aunt Margie intervened, "Sweetie, you've been out of touch with Connie for five months. The last time you called her was your check-in back in March. You missed April, and then she thought you might have forgotten and waited through May. She's been on a mission to bring you home since at least then."

Sophia smiled. "I don't know what I'm supposed to do. Come inside see what I've done to the cabin".

It was a strange feeling. One that strangled her breath and hurt her stomach. Shouldn't she feel joy or relief? Her smile faded. She led Connie and the others into the small cabin. She had covered the walls with braided grasses framed with twigs that she bound with vine fibers, and a dried deer hide acted as a rug between the bed and counter. The cast-iron skillet hung on the wall by the woodstove. A small stack of wood was tucked in the corner by the fireplace behind the rocker.

"You're here to take me away?"

Winston ran out and greeted Connie and Aunt Margie.

"Please, Sissie, I can't live not knowing if you're alive from one day to the next. Come home with me. I'm begging you."

"Sophia," Margie soothed. "This is yours. You can visit as much as you like. But Connie's right. Your family needs you. This cabin has been going for a hundred years. It'll wait for you." The older woman took in the decorations and modern systems. "This stuff is meant to last. Go home, get some rest, and bring the people you love. This kind of beauty needs to be shared." She squeezed Sophia's shoulders.

Sophia picked up Ethel as she ran in the open door and tucked her under her arm. She was a sizable 4-pound blackbird, now. She laid eggs that kept Sophia going when the fish stopped biting, and the jerky ran out. She loved her new life. But the winters were hard. Some nights kept her up, thinking the whole forest was going to tumble down on her and the little cabin.

"You can bring your chicken," Connie urged.

Sophia nodded. She made her peace and learned to respect mother nature. In doing so, her state of awareness proved that all life was precious—from Mitch, her beloved red squirrel to the trout that fed many a forest creature. There was balance. "I came to find myself," she said to the faces in the small space.

"I had no idea who Sophia Stevens was, let alone what she wanted. But I'm not that woman anymore. I came to prove to myself that I could live on my own and survive. I can do anything I set my mind to and flourish. I am at peace with myself now and can go back to civilization. I'm ready for whatever the world is going to dish out to me now. I'm ready for another adventure—one where I can share my knowledge. People need to know how to embrace what we have with respect. Conservancy and protection aren't words. They are power. Power in the hands of children as they grow. We are all children learning. If I could leave my home in California to live in a one-room cabin in the mountains of Idaho, others can do the same."

The ranger left to check out the water collection bin beneath the rain gutter she had fashioned from a hallowed tree. The outhouse had a bouquet of dried wildflowers attached to the door with a bent nail. Sophia had managed to build a storage shed to house her food supply. And Sophia's Jeep CJ5 served as a pantry. There were mason jars of preserved foods from the harvest the prior summer. Folded clothes laying on the front seat looked laundered. Sophia was thriving. Though hungry for more than eggs and pantry foods, she was better off than some of the homesteaders and preppers he'd rescued in the weeks prior. One man even lost his life.

"You had one heck of a teacher, Ms. Stevens," the ranger praised.

Sophia stood proud. "I had the best, my husband, Jonathan."

***

Before she left the cabin, Sophia noticed the lake surface was calm and reflected the sunrise like glass on a mirror. It was her looking glass. The one that held the secrets to her adventure tucked away in the magical wood of the Coeur d'Alene mountains—a place where time stood still. It taught her that she was braver than she knew and tougher than she believed. "Even Alice had to go back through the looking glass," she whispered, "because all adventures have an end."

Chapter 15
REUNION

The ranger's station disappeared around the bend as Sophia watched through the rearview window of her Jeep CJ5. Aunt Margie sat in the passenger seat while Connie and her husband followed. It was an eight-hour ride back to their house. They lived in a rural area with ten or fewer houses on the 20 mile trip to town. The golden hayfields blew in the gentle summer heat. The bright green leaves of the potato plants offered a great contrast. It had been twenty-two months since Sophia had seen anything outside the small town back in the mountains.

Sophia no longer felt the rush and pull that society and culture placed on the inhabitants. It did not matter if she drove through Boise or California. The fact was— she had changed. People would forever bustle to their schedules, forced to keep steadfast by their perceptions of themselves. Had she stayed, she too would still be rushing, making appointments for everything from lunch with friends to manicures and house cleaners. But being in the woods taught her that there was no hurry. It was an illusion placed before her; everyone.

She pulled into her sister's driveway, her niece and nephew bouncing toward the Jeep CJ5. Aunt Margie climbed from her side, eager to greet the smiling kindergarten-aged pair. Sophia removed Ethel's crate from the backseat and held it in front of her. She knew the kids would notice, and that would be the end of all reunions. Ethel was going to steal the show. She was sure Winston wouldn't mind.

"Eh, hmm," she cleared her throat to bring attention to the crate, a genuine smile on her face. Something she learned was a gift. To smile when something pleases you is not the same as smiling from anticipated joy. Also, it takes more muscles to frown than to smile. Great for her, no more aging face, she thought.

She was not disappointed. The children turned their head enough to see the white plastic carrier and bounced toward Ethel while Winston licked their faces to say hello.

She was not disappointed. The children turned their heads enough to see the white plastic carrier and bounced toward Ethel.

"What is it?" they squealed in unison.

"This is my pet chicken. Her name is Ethel. Be gentle; she's a little nervous." Sophia laughed. "And she's fast."

Connie's place was on ten acres with fields around, so Sophia felt comfortable letting Ethel out of her crate. She set it down on the dirt driveway and opened the door. Ethel stepped into the sunlit dirt and grass. She was raised in the woods. The new surroundings sent her back into the crate. But only for a moment. She wandered back out and then pecked her way into the yard with the duo following close behind, their giggles filling the air.

"You domesticated a chicken?" Sophia's brother-in-law asked, teasing, not expecting an answer.

"What can I say? I liked her feathers," Sophia teased back. It felt good to interact. To be among laughing. It felt good stretching out her metaphorical wings beyond the boundary of her small plot of woods.

"My flight to LAX leaves at seven tomorrow, I'm going to visit some old friends and see if I like California. But for now, I'm going to head inside. Connie was kind enough to lend me your room." Aunt Margie winked, then wrapped her arms around Sophia for the first time since seeing her. "I was so worried about you, missy. I'm glad to have you safe."

Sophia smiled and nodded. It was uncomfortable receiving words of love and worry. It would have been warranted had she thought she was in danger, but it hadn't donned on her that she was cut-off. That without Connie, no one would have thought to look for her. "Thank you," she whispered to the older woman.

"I see they found Ethel."

"Looks like it." Sophia watched as the chicken dodged the kids, weaving through the yard. "If you sit, she might come to you," she called.

The twins sat. Ethel stopped running to study them. Winston took advantage and toppled them with kisses.

Connie came up behind Sophia. "You know, you don't have to go back to California."

"But Connie," Sophia protested.

"Sis, think about it. You're all welcome here. Hell, we could even go back to the cabin at times. There's no rush to go back to your old life."

Sophia turned to study her chicken, not unlike Ethel to the twins. *What kept me away?* she thought. She still had Jack wrapped in fabric in the front console of the car. "Connie, I needed closure, and I had to do it my way.

Jonathan and I had plans for a long retirement. He never made it to forty. We made a promise to go on living and exploring. In my head, that meant finishing our plans. You know we traveled. We went RVing, camping, off-roading. Our life was filled with adventure, yes. But what it held was appreciation and respect for nature. We shared meteor showers beneath the desert sky, walked through forests where wildlife lived free and uninhibited. The cabin was our long-term plan. The timeline for rebuilding the house in Cali gave me a chance to take a sabbatical. To live out those plans, our dreams. I won't deny I was naïve. Life off-grid is hard when you're alone. Mine was only beginning. Some people do it for the rest of their lives."

Ethel clucked, drawing Sophia and Connie's attention back to the kids. They patted her head and rubbed over her neck feathers. Ethel strutted away and then back to them. Her unease mimicked Sophia's.

Connie took her sister's hand. "At least stay until the house is finished. We went out there a few times as you asked. It's not for the faint of heart. If you want to stay here, you could always put one of those tiny homes in the back lot."

Sophia's niece ran up to her with Ethel in her arms. "Look, Aunt Sophia, she trusts me." Ethel tucked her legs in and settled in the child's arms. "She's so soft."

"I'll stay until the house is done. I think I'm ready for the next chapter in the book of Sophia." She smiled and bumped her sister's shoulder. "Yeah, I'm ready."

* * *

It was the day for her to return to her rebuilt home in California.

Sophia kissed the twins and hugged her sister.

"Go on, you'll be fine," Connie teased. "Don't hesitate to come back. If you can't do it or if you don't want to—"

"I don't want to, Con, but I have to." Sophia blew her sister a kiss and rolled up the window.

Connie waved from the end of the driveway until the Jeep CJ5 disappeared in the distance.

Chapter 16

HOME

Sophia stopped at the entrance of the development. The last time she was there, the trees were black protrusions in a marred landscape. The housing lots were littered with twisted appliances and debris. Cars had the paint burned off them, roof racks melted, and tires gone. Swimming pools were filled with ash-laden water. That was two years ago.

"It felt like an eternity," she said to Jack.

The ground was covered in lush greens like she had never seen. They were bright, a green that pierced the landscape and showed new life—rebirth. Jonathan had told her about the miracle of nature. He'd said, "Fire is hard. It takes no prisoners, but there's a secret few people know. There are beetles that rely on wildfires. They have heat sensors that draw them from miles away to feast on the burned trees. And then there are plants like the Bush Mallows that have seed banks which remain dormant for over a hundred years." She smiled, remembering his excitement. "Sophe, sometimes what we see as a tragedy is another's means to survive."

Tears moistened her lashes as she remembered his words. His voice was a ghost. A tone lost to time. She longed to hear him, one more time. She took Jack from his spot, nestled in the fabric nest she fashioned for him, intent on keeping it—him safe. She put him in her white parka pocket and continued further into the development. Winding around the twists and turns through new homes and construction projects, she gasped. There were young landscapes and mini-mansions, bi-levels and architectural wonders, and empty lots, void of it all.

She knew the bend ahead. It was theirs. She slowed the Jeep CJ5 to a crawl. It had taken all she had to give up her new life in Idaho. There were new memories and emotions attached to the cabin. The past two years, she discovered how not just to survive but to live. To enjoy the smallest moments. Coming back to California was another awakening. One that she didn't want but needed. Perhaps what she told Connie was true—it was closure or maybe reassurance. Reassurance that it was all real. For even in the forest, cut off from the world, it all still felt like a dream.

It was easy living in a dream. There was nothing to force you to wake, even if a flood kept you from the easy life. *But what was easy,* she wondered. *Loving someone with all my heart was easy. It was realizing what a precious man he was and how his love of all things lives on through me. It is that which is easy.*

She kept the pressure steady on the accelerator. The Jeep CJ5 climbed the hill and rounded the bend with ease. Sophia's heart drummed in her chest. Winston whined and sniffed the air. She clenched the wheel. *Almost there,* she thought. Then, with a painful breath, she accelerated to finish the climb. She turned left and rolled to her destination.

Sophia pulled the Jeep CJ5 into the resin bond driveway. Her hands shook as she put the vehicle in park. It took her a moment to gather the gumption. She opened the door and stepped out onto the Resin Bound gravel driveway, This was the environmentally friendly natural material which she chose instead of asphalt. This is one of the most permeable driving surfaces on the market, as the gap between the aggregate materials remains open, enabling water to drain away with ease. This was only one of many features Sophia chose for her new home. *Lets see the rest,* she thought, excited to check out everything.

She took Jack from her pocket and clutched him to her chest with both hands. Winston followed at her side.

The grass was green and new—sod. The cement walkway gleamed white in the California sun. Several young conifers stood tall among a myriad of other shrubs. She had left the choosing to the landscaper. The white path led to a massive red fiberglass door, another sustainable low energy feature. It stood out against the white stucco ranch with clay shingles. Even the rooftop had the solar panels she desired. This house was made entirely Green, with all sustainable features, as a tribute to Jonathon's love for the environment. She took a deep, cleansing breath and stepped up to the door. She punched in her code, the one the security company gave her, and opened the door. Winston stayed by her side as they stepped over the threshold together, her best friend, into the hunter green and bamboo living room; she kissed the orange knife and whispered, "Babe, we're home."

*****

SURVIVAL LISTS

Know and research your location.
Know your surroundings.
Prepare for the environment you live in.

··

Preparing for survival in an earthquake, wildfire, tornado, hurricane, flood, mudslide, etc....any natural disaster is critical. Don't wait for the emergency. It will be too late.

I invite you to use my lists as a guide to creating your own unique survival lists. These are the lists that I have been compiling throughout the years. I have survived major earthquakes, wildfires, hurricanes, thunderstorms, and flash-floods while camping and living in Northern and Southern California. This list may be just a start for you. It may also provide items/things you've never thought about. As we know, technology and new-fangled items appear on the market daily, and yet, so quickly the list is out-of-date. These lists are by all means not complete. This is a straight-forward, simple list of items I know you will find handy. Surviving a natural disaster, or preparing to live off grid is the best way to prepare for you and your family's safety.

This has been a passion of my late husband Mark. I continue to add to these lists and hope you will find value in this compilation. Have a back-up plan which includes if one car does not start, have another one ready to go... AND be sure to take the obvious, your purse with ID and wallet. In the 2017 Northern California wildfires, I grabbed everything I could for everyone else in my family and I forgot myself. When I was evacuated from my home, I forgot my purse and ID and the First Responders would not let me go back to my house for a week. It was horrible because I needed my ID. Please check, double and triple check! And even the most prepared folks still might forget something. Enjoy!

The same is true if you are planning a vacation, if you are going on a hike or a camping trip.

In my book I list the main requirements for off grid living:

1. You must have a generator with any source of fuel: gasoline, propane, or solar

2. A sewage collection system has to be in place, an outhouse, or a compost toilet

3. Water has to be accessible

4. Think about your food source with ways to irrigate and plant seeds and reuse water

5. Cutting tools are necessary to be able to make items and process food

Locate food, water, shelter; secure your perimeter.
Familiarize yourself with your surroundings.

SUPPLIES FOR SURVIVAL:

1. Know your plan, tell a family member where you plan to go, plan a designated time for an occasional check-in

2. Find local store or post office at your destination to have family/loved ones know where to send you a message, check that location if you are on a long road trip

3. Keep a list of emergency contacts in a notebook (paper copy and digital copy emailed to a family/friend)

4. Have paper maps and highlighted multiple routes color-coded

5. Include your physician, fire, hospital, sheriff/police departments on the map

6. List should include hotels/campgrounds, pet-friendly if needed

7. Keep a bag of important documents ready (paper and digital)

8. Photos of family members including your pets, put names and info on the back of each photo.

9. Advanced medical directive for you, each family member and your pets (what to do and approved expenses for each family member and pet)

10. Keep a copy of medical records for all family members including blood types and allergies

11. Keep your car(s) fueled up/charged at all times, you never know when you need to go

12. Have a network of people to go to/people to call/friend/ family members to contact

13. Have a bug-out bag for each person in your family including each pet

14. Food, water and meds for 5-7 days if evacuating

15. Food, water and meds for 14 days minimum if sheltering in place

16. Pet carrier folding wire cage

....

Create a sign (ready to post if necessary) stating names, locations of animals when evacuating an area of natural disaster

....

BUG-OUT BAG CONTENTS:

1. Pack the most important items, pack light, yet pack things that have multiple uses. Remember, get the smallest, thinnest items that work

2. Main items to keep in mind: maintain bodily functions, combustion devices, clothing for core temperature control (can be thin and lightweight), containers for food and cutting items

3. Astronaut blanket (thin and very tiny)

4. Solar charger and cords that fit your devices (pack correct adapters; some are faster charging than other adapters and not compatible) Get a small one

5. Mirror, whistle, compass

6. Emergency crank radio/solar radio

7. First Aid kit with butterfly bandages (compact for bug-out bag as well as full set)

8. First Aid kit dedicated to skin irritations such as poison oak and poison ivy, poisonous plants, reversal medications, topical cleansers, ointments, anti-itch

9. Basic can opener, canned food

10. Small soap, toilet paper

11. Rope/carabiner/work gloves that are snug

12. Scarf

13. Survival bracelet with knife made of woven rope for emergency

14. Water purification supplies like Life Straw, UV water treatment or iodine tablets

15. Water bottle/camel pack insert for backpack

16. One rolled up change of clothes: sweatshirt, pants, underwear, socks

17. Sun hat, baseball cap, and beanie

18. Head lamp

19. GO PRO/Recording device if you have room

20. A retractable pole, hooks, lures, and sinkers for fishing

21. Batteries: AAA, AA, 9V, C, D

22. Ammo (small bag, assorted sizes)

23. Ammo adapter (any size will fit the 12-gauge with adapters)

24. A knife, pocket knife

25. Chewing gum

26. Duct tape

27. Flares

28. Glow sticks

29. Magnesium firestarter

30. Matches

31. Fire can also be started using hand sanitizer, cotton balls/Q-tips, and lighter

32. Small, blow-up camp pillow

33. Mess kit (spork, collapsible cup, small liquid dish soap dispenser, and cut square of scotch cleaning pad)

34. Power bar/energy gummies/trail mix

35. Earplugs

36. Pet's list (food, bowls, medication, brushes, etc.)

37. Pocket-size forestry book

38. Pencils, paper, pens

39. Paper clips

40. Small personal kit: toothpaste, toothbrush, comb/brush, tweezers, nail clipper, nail file

41. Have paper maps and highlighted multiple routes (color-coded)

42. Camp towel

43. Sunscreen, SPF lip balm, 2 pairs of socks, water shoes, sunglasses

44. Collapsible mini-lantern

45. Ziploc bags

46. Disposable feet/hand warmer

47. PPE, face mask, goggles

48. Cash

49. Glasses

50. Medications

51. Consider Gatorade powder

52. Nunn Hydration, EmerGen-C, probiotics, activated supplements

53. Jetboil, portable cooking system (if you have room)

54. Mini-straps to add the pet pack to your pack

55. Field guide for tracking game; mini-field guide on edible plants and animal tracking local to the area with area map

56. Field dressing kit, pack of salt, pepper, and sugar, garlic and Ziploc bag (to get the fleas out of animal fur)

SURVIVAL ITEMS FOR THE CAR

(Consider a bug-out bag for each car you own)

1. HAM radio, solar hand crank radio
2. Bucket/folding/collapsible camp chair
3. Shotgun/rifle/handgun, ammo, ammo adapter in the car you are going to take
4. Freeze dried food for 1 week
5. Machete (larger knife)
6. Water can
7. PPE, gloves, masks, disinfectant wipes
8. Paper towel rolls
9. Toilet paper rolls
10. Towels
11. Extra jacket, snow hat, gloves
12. Snow scraper
13. Auto oil/transmission fluid
14. Fuel can
15. All-in-one tool kit
16. Car fuses
17. Tire pump/gauge
18. Spray paint
19. Flares

20. Jumper cables/battery-powered jumper cables

21. Compact shovel

22. Learn how to change your tires and replace battery

23. Remember your bug-out bag for each member of your family and pet

REPAIR LIST:

1. Tarp

2. Fuel: gas, diesel, propane, oil (whatever your emergency equipment needs to work)

3. Battery

4. Jumper cables

5. Shovel

6. Hammer, wrench, pliers

7. Nails, screws

8. Screwdrivers, reg and phillip's

9. All-in-one tool

10. Duct tape

11. Super glue/glue

12. Zip ties

13. Saw

14. Pencils

15. Manual air pump with adapters

16. Axe

17. Leather work gloves

18. Basic sewing kit

LIVING WITHOUT ELECTRICITY LIST:

1. Hand sanitizer and Vaseline (doubles as a firestarter)

2. Candles and flashlight, headlamp for hands-free lighting

3. Cotton balls

4. Batteries and battery charger

5. Gas and diesel

6. Propane tanks filled (small and larger size)

7. Generator (there are many types fueled by solar, propane, electric, natural gas, gasoline, diesel)

8. Solar water heater kit

9. Laundry hand washer

10. Manual chainsaw with hand straps

11. Solar outdoor shower kit

12. Mobile solar panels

13. Compost bin

14. Compost toilet

15. Buckets

16. Source for water

17. Back up ways to clean water

18. Extra wood bundles

19. Canned food

20. Freeze dried food

PET LIST: Prepare for Pets/Animal Evacuation

1. Microchip your pets; ID tags on all pets/animals

2. Never leave animals locked in barns, sheds or cages/ kennels

3. Prep equines by turning them out into a safe defensible space. Do not turn animals loose where they can get onto the roads or become hazards to responders

4. Make an ID wearable tag for all animals

5. Create and post a whiteboard or sign listing all animals and locations.

6. Know who to call

7. Create a neighborhood animal evac buddy network and get to know each other's animals

8. Set out a hide-a-key and tell loved one where it is

PET BUG-OUT BAG:

1. Food, water and meds for 5-7 days if evacuating (Minimum of 14 days if sheltering in place)

2. Pet carrier folding wire cage

3. Journal, pens, pencils

4. List of pet-friendly motels, Airbnb, friends, relatives, campsites

5. Freeze dried food, kibble

6. Collar, name and copy of Vet records, current vaccines, and number of your vet for emergency.

7. Current license, registrations for your pet/animal

8. Advance care directives and how much to spend and what to do with your pet/animal in case if emergency

9. Line up help before you need it—create a network of neighbors who are familiar with your pet

10. Know who to call

11. Toy, fold-up bowls

12. Water can with silicone bowl attachment

13. First aid pet kit

14. Grooming supplies

15. Wipes

16. Can opener, fork/spoon, plastic lid

17. Cool pads, ice pack

18. Poop bags, diaper, kennel pads

19. Disposable litter pan and litter in Ziploc

20. Ziploc bags

21. Pet-safe disinfectant and cleaning supplies

22. Sheet and towels for pet privacy

23. Pet bedding

24. Calming aids, ThunderShirt

25. Treats and toys

26. Animal-safe disinfectants and cleaning supplies

LIST OF PET TO-DOS FOR EACH ANIMAL:

1. Make sure pets are secured in cars so they don't jump out

2. Make sure to have secure accommodations at your evac location

3. Many pets escape from their evac locations and are then lost in unfamiliar surroundings, take extra precautions

4. Enough food, water & medications for 7-10 days

5. Pack a halter, lead rope, collar, harness, leash for each animal

6. Carriers, cages

7. Reflective collar

8. Large pillow case (Makes a good temporary carrier for cats, bird, reptiles)

IN CASE OF EVACUATIONS: Know your surroundings

1. Post your sign for location, name of all pets on the front door

2. Turn off AC

3. Unplug appliances

4. Leave a posted note on your front door for first responders— people/animals who left or remain on premises

5. Practice loading animals in the day and night and in a variety of trailers

6. Have multiple options for everything

7. Keep cars fueled at all times

8. Prepare for new location with lots of potable water

9. Prepare safe spaces

10. Close windows

11. Leave doors unlocked or key hidden

12. Don't wait for mandatory evacuation orders

13. Create a neighborhood phone tree and practice emergency calling

14. Don't request help from unauthorized social media groups

··

Remember to let loved ones know where your destination will be. Check in if the plan changes.

··

FOR ANIMALS SHELTERING IN PLACE:

1. Disable electric gates, and garage doors

2. Dispose of electrical gates and garage door

3. Post signs listing animals, use your already created signs and pet locations

4. Make sure address is clearly visible

5. Close windows

6. Leave doors unlocked or key hidden

7. Leave lots of water

8. Turn off A/C and unplug appliances

9. Don't wait for mandatory evacuation orders

10. Don't request help from unauthorized social media groups

11. Leave a message on voicemail for local authorities if you are leaving an animal(s)

12. Do not post photos or videos of injured animals, destroyed property or people rescuing animals

13. DO NOT attempt to rescue wild animals

IDAHO WILD LIFE: Plants and Forestry

Edibles (this is information about Idaho that I wrote in my story)

1. Stinging nettles
2. Fern shoots
3. Sap from a pine tree
4. Pine nuts
5. Wild strawberries
6. Fireweed (High in vitamin C)
7. Morels
8. Huckleberries,
9. Hawthorn fruits
10. Cattail roots
11. Serviceberry stem (these have been used in Native medicinal practices for centuries)
12. Refreshing leaves of the field mint

···

Learn about the edible plants and wild life where you live.

···

WAYS TO START A FIRE:

1. Any petroleum has oil to start fire
2. Starter material like a cotton ball or dry kindling

3. Hand sanitizer

4. Lip balm with petroleum

5. Matches

6. Stick and wood with string (if you need instructions, watch YouTube videos)

7. Lighter

8. Magnesium shavings/firestarter

OFF GRID WATER PURIFICATION METHODS:

1. DIY Bio-filters

2. UV/sunlight purification systems

3. Ceramic filters

4. Chemical (bleach) disinfectant

5. Distillation

6. Boiling

7. 13-gallon LifeStraw option

8. Boiling hot rocks

9. Dirt filtration through a scarf

10. Use of gray water for watering plants, recycle water as much as possible

LIST FOR WINTER NEEDS

1. Creosote logs to be burned every week
2. Wood supply needs to have dry wood to burn
3. Holding tank for water
4. Compost bin
5. Extra dog kibble
6. Sugar
7. Chicken feed
8. Fire extinguisher
9. Snow shoes
10. Feet/hand warmers
11. Beanie cap
12. Mason jars for canning summer food
13. All the supplies that are listed in my survival checkoff
14. Pet sweaters/coats
15. Waterproof clothing for everyone

TYPES OF GENERATORS:

1. Solar generator: example Yeti Zero, the largest one to date as of 2021-the 6000x plus portable solar panels
2. Gas generator
3. Propane generator
4. Natural gas generator

DRESSING BIG GAME

1. Get the fleas off the fur—with small game place in a zip lock bag and seal

2. For big game not much you can do with removal of the fleas and ticks from the fur

3. Use all of the organs for fishing, feeding pets, food supply

4. Drain the blood

5. Smoke meat

6. Hang chunks of meat to dry in a protected shed

7. Skin and tan the hide

8. Melt the bear fat to make bear oil: use empty food cans for storage, canning for cooking, lubrication of guns and knives, preserving leather, burning fuel in oil lamps, and in some cultures for forecasting the weather

....

A Green House is an environmentally friendly house with solar panels and battery for storage.

....

GREEN LIVING: Your checklist for an environmentally friendly home

1. Window treatments

2. Use Green appliances

3. Energy efficiency lighting

4. Reduce your water use

5. Clean air conditioner

6. Keep your garden Green - creating compost is a great way to keep your garden even greener with its multiple eco-friendly benefits. Scraps such as eggshells, fruit and vegetable peels, tea bags, and stale bread are the perfect food for your compost pile and can improve the health of your soil while giving back to the environment and controlling household waste.

7. Reuse gray water for gardening or flushing toilet but not for potable water source

8. Fiberglass door, sustainable low energy feature

9. Stucco

10. Clay Shingles

11. Resin bound gravel driveway - natural material instead of asphalt, one of the most permeable driving surfaces (enables water to drain away with ease and absorb into the ground)

RESOURCES

INTERNET

Merriam-Webster.com Dictionary s.v. "processed"
https://www.merriam-webster.com/dictionary/processed.

What to do Before, During and After a Wildfire
https://www.fire.ca.gov/media/5414/beforeduringafter.pdf

Shotgun Adapters
https://www.gunadapters.com/

Proenneke's Cabin in Alaska
https://www.nps.gov/lacl/learn/historyculture/proennekes-cabin.htm

Idaho Plants and Wildlife
https://www.fs.usda.gov/detail/ipnf/maps
pubs/?cid=fsm9_019115

Essential Gear for Off Grid Living
https://www.popularmechanics.com/adventure/outdoor-gear/g27631930/off-the-grid-tools/

Types of Generators for Off Grid Living
https://www.architecturelab.net/types-of-generators/

Goal Zero Generator
https://www.goalzero.com/shop/archive-power/goal-zero-yeti-1250-portable-power-station/

Water Purification Off Grid

https://maximumoffgrid.com/off-grid-water-systems/off-grid-water-filtration-purification/

How to Make Bear Grease

https://www.themeateater.com/cook/butchering-and-processing/how-to-make-bear-grease

Resin Bound Gravel Driveways

https://www.homelogicdriveways.co.uk/what-is-suds-drainage

Creating an Environmentally Friendly Home

https://www.sepco-solarlighting.com/blog/green-living-your-checklist-creating-an-environmentally-friendly-home

Personal Wild Fire Action Plan (created by CAL fire)

www.fire.ca.gov

YOUTUBE VIDEOS

Defensible spaces - protecting your home from wildfire

Earthquake - securing your surroundings

Resilient landscaping

Evacuation checklists

BOOKS

The best series of books that I've found from a single source is Dave Canterbury's collection of Bushcraft

1. **Bushcraft 101A Field Guide to the Art of Wilderness Survival** by Dave Canterbury

2. **Bushcraft First Aid** by Dave Canterbury and Jason Hunt, PhD

3. **The Bushcraft Field Guide to Trapping, Gathering, and Cooking in the Wild** by Dave Canterbury

4. **Advanced Bushcraft** by Dave Canterbury

5. **Bushcraft boxed collection** by Dave Canterbury and Jason Hunt (*this is a series of books designed for survival that I highly recommend*)

6. **A Landowner's Guide to Managing Your Woods: How to Maintain a Small Acreage for Long-Term Health, Biodiversity, and High-Quality Timber Production** by Hansen, Severson and Waterman

··

Stay Informed, Stay Safe
··

ABOUT THE AUTHOR

Kimberly Quan Hubenette, DDS, is an accomplished dentist and a survivor. At the early age of 18, she knew she wanted to become a doctor of dental surgery. Whatever she does she does it with her full energy. Her parents, Anna and William, ingrained upon her that she could be anything she wanted to achieve and she grew up believing it. Born in Santa Monica, California, raised in the small, rural, border town of El Centro, California, she grew up in her Chinese American household, not knowing she was anything else but a human being. Without color, race or culture holding her back, her American born Chinese parents tried very hard to assimilate in the American/ Chinese/ Mexican culture. She is the third generation of Chinese American descent in her family tree.

Kimberly grew up hunting, shooting, fishing, off roading, 4x4ing with her parents and siblings, Derek and Gregory. Her family belonged to off road 4-wheel drive club and had three wheelers, trailers, and trucks. Her father's best friends were in Search and Rescue, and her dad has always been a survivalist as well. He used to train Kim how to survive an attack, in home invasion and kept survival gear in every car. Being attracted to that, lead her to meet her late husband, Mark, who is the rest of the perfect love story. He was her soul mate, and she moved to be with him to Kenwood, California. Uprooted from her family for the first time, the 10-hour drive was difficult at first, yet, their lifestyle was the same as she had known it growing up.

Mark Hubenette was her inspiration for writing this novel based on a true story. As a widow, Kimberly has surpassed surviving. She is an active member of her community in which she works, Sonoma. She is a health and fitness and anti-aging buff, always up on the cutting edge of dental technology, and whole-body health. She has the CANI Philosophy (Constant And Never-Ending Improvement) and loves to mentor friends, staff, and community on life. Being the best you can be to yourself, others and environment is her mantra. Her commitment to her friends and patients is bountiful. She can sense when someone needs her, and often feels what her good friends are feeling even hundreds of miles away. For example, her eye was twitching and it turned out her friend had an eye-altering situation.

Kimberly has a growing bucket list that she is checking off as time goes on. Items that she has had on this list, like catching a large wahoo fish, hiking Half Dome in Yosemite, and camping with her beloved dog Dakota on their weekly journeys keeps her life busy. She enjoys her outdoor lifestyle and encourages everyone to incorporate open fresh air as much as possible and to get out and walk or hike daily. She continues to reinvent herself to be true to life with her friends and family in Northern and Southern California.

INSPIRATION

I am inspired by my own personal journey of life; Knowing I can achieve anything I set my mind to. Life is what you make of it. Don't sit on your couch and sulk thinking life has dealt you a bad hand.

Pick Yourself Up and Shake the Dust Off!

For a brief moment I felt I could not go on after my husband passed holding my hand after a long battle of Cystic Fibrosis; a 21-year survivor of a double lung transplant. He was a happy-go-lucky type of guy. Even his longtime family physician kept seeing him and was one of three remaining long-time patients that Dr. Chris Brown would see in his director role at CPMC, San Francisco. Dr. Brown was his friend and confidant, and Mark often referred to him as Chris, but never to his face. He respected his doctor, and called him Dr. Brown. Mark had his cell phone, and refused to use it. In the 30 years of being his patient, he only used it three times.

After the 2017 Wildfires struck our neighborhood of Santa Rosa/ Northern California, Mark, had to be on constant oxygen. Even with this new condition, he never gave up on life. He was an 8-year volunteer team member with Sonoma County Search and Rescue and still helped his team with search and rescue on that event. He was an animal tracker, held a ham radio license, First Responder, first-aid certifications, and had an affinity towards all animals. He could understand all animals.

During the 2017 Fires, Mark was on the dispatch radio duty because none of his team mates wanted him to go outside, due to his lungs. But the soot and the poor air quality for months afterward, caught up with my Mark. He never was able to live life fully thereafter. He did not have the strength to ride his motorcycle, his razor, or go RVing after that devastating loss of environment. He was a fighter and I believe he lasted far beyond what anyone with his conditions could have (47 years) because he never took no for an answer.

His parents, Bill and Tish, are the ones that instilled this upon him. They never treated him differently, and he never wanted to be treated different. He never gave up. He had few friends. However, the few he had were treated like gold. He would do anything for his true friends. And they, in return, would do anything for him as well. His oldest friend Tim and brother Sean, were his childhood neighbors, His "brother from a different mother", Frank, and his gaming friends Richard AKA, "Jehooty" and wife

Amanda are examples of friends for life. Our neighbors Spencer and Andy Brady would come visit him at the hospital all hours of the night. His three best friends, Eric, Tim and Todd would facetime him nightly until the last day, even when he could no longer speak, they kept calling. They were the ones who were there for his transplant and were there for his death.